D0340185

ROSE SEES RED

ROSE

SEES RED

Cecil Castellucci

Scholastic Press
New York

Copyright © 2010 by Cecil Castellucci

All rights reserved. Published by Scholastic Press, an imprint of Scholastic Inc., *Publishers since 1920*. SCHOLASTIC, SCHOLASTIC PRESS, and associated logos are trademarks and/or registered trademarks of Scholastic Inc.

No part of this publication may be reproduced, stored in a retrieval system, or transmitted in any form or by any means, electronic, mechanical, photocopying, recording, or otherwise, without written permission of the publisher. For information regarding permission, write to Scholastic Inc., Attention: Permissions Department, 557 Broadway, New York, NY 10012.

Library of Congress Cataloging-in-Publication Data
Castellucci, Cecil, 1969–
    Rose sees red / Cecil Castellucci. — 1st ed.
        p. cm.
    Summary: In the 1980s, two teenage ballet dancers — one American, one Russian — spend an unforgettable night in New York City, forming a lasting friendship despite their cultural and political differences.
    ISBN 978-0-545-06079-0 (hardcover)
    [1. Ballet dancing — Fiction.   2. Friendship — Fiction.   3. Russians — New York (State) — New York — Fiction.   4. New York (N.Y.) — History — 20th century — Fiction.] I. Title.
    PZ7.C26865Ro 2010
    [Fic] — dc22

                                                                         2009036850

10 9 8 7 6 5 4 3 2 1   10 11 12 13 14

Printed in the U.S.A.   23
First edition, August 2010

The text was set in Goudy Old Style.
Book design by Becky Terhune.

for

Lise, Vincent & Laurent Castellucci, with love and gratitude,

and those friends (especially Andrea Kleine, Nancy Ross, and Melissa Auf der Maur) who helped me find a way back

Thank you.

The Walk Down the Hill

I was black inside and so I took everything black.

Toast.

Coffee.

Clothes.

Heart.

It was the end of October, and a few leaves were still clinging on to the trees, all bright yellow, red, and orange. These leaves were suckers, I thought, tricking themselves into thinking that this fall would be different, that they wouldn't have to let go and turn brown and make room for snow.

That's what I had done. Before I was black, I was like them. I had tricked myself, at the end of summer, into thinking that starting high school would somehow make everything different. That I would be reinvented. That I would find my true friends. But it was almost Halloween and I was still lonely and friendless, and that made me see everything with a dark point of view.

Everyone in my family could tell I had a black cloud over me. I wore it like an extra sweater.

"We're worried about you, Rose," my mom said across the table while I barely ate my toast.

She said it all the time, and every time it made my chest tighten. I felt bad that she was worried, but there wasn't anything I could do about it except mumble that I was doing just fine.

"What?" she said. "I can't hear you."

"I'm fine," I said again. But I knew she was unconvinced.

My dad dealt with it by sinking deeper behind his *New York Times*. My brother, Todd, tried to make jokes, but he seemed to be the only one who ever laughed.

Maybe he just wasn't funny.

"Come on, let's rock and roll," Todd said this time, grabbing an extra banana for the walk down to the bus stop.

"Have a good day at school," Mom said. As I passed her to leave, she squeezed my shoulder. She wanted to give me a little encouragement, but I couldn't let anything in.

"Rose," she said, pulling me back into the kitchen. She put the palm of her hand on my face and cupped it.

Her hand was warm, and I could feel something. I could feel that she was trying to send me some love.

In science class, Mrs. Merrick said that in outer space if you move one inch, you could end up a million miles out of your way.

And that's what had happened to me.

"Mom," I said, shaking her off.

It was a good thing, my mother's warm hand on my face. Standing at the front door with the cold nip in the air, I could still feel it.

As soon as I got outside, I motioned at the two men in suits who always hung out on the street corner in front of our house. They were like overgrown, well-dressed delinquents.

"What do you think—KGB or CIA?" I asked Todd.

It was no secret that our neighborhood in Riverdale was crawling with KGB and CIA agents. You'd think the Bronx would be the farthest thing away from the Cold War, but next door to us was the Soviet apartment compound.

Here, on a daily basis, I was reminded that the superpowers were acting like a couple of stupid kids on a playground. Only they were messing with the whole world.

"You can tell who's who by their eyebrows," Todd said, his usual goofy self. But then he stopped dead in his tracks, like he always did whenever the girl next door walked down her front steps.

She was a vision. I'll give him that. Her legs were impossibly long and lean, and when she walked, it looked as though she were gliding. Her steps were so impossibly sure of themselves. Regal.

"Oh my *Goddess*," Todd said.

Todd really did think that the girl next door was a Goddess. He had even rolled up a Deity that looked just like her to use as a Non-Player Character in the Dungeons and Dragons game he ran in our garage every Friday night.

I swear he wanted to bow to her.

I didn't say anything, though. I waited for him because I knew he always waited for me no matter how much I dragged my feet, or gave him dirty looks, or lived under the black cloud. Every morning he still walked me down the hill to the bus stop.

He did it out of love. He did it out of a brotherly sense of chivalry. We both knew that if he didn't go with me I would have to stand at the bus stop alone, and even if we didn't talk to each other, I must admit that it was a comfort to have him there.

"They have a school in the Soviet compound," Todd said, and he pointed over to the large white apartment building down the street on Fieldston Road. "That's where she's going to school. She doesn't have to live in the compound because her dad's a Communist bigwig. That's why they get to be in the townhouse next door."

Todd's obsession with the girl next door knew no bounds. One could even say that he spied on her, because he accumulated what information he had and told it to me whenever he was reminded of her existence.

"She's sixteen. From Moscow. She just got her hair cut. She speaks French as well as she speaks English. She's a ballet dancer like you. She likes strawberry ice cream. She listens to The Police."

My room looked out into hers—the townhouses we lived in shared a garden path. I'd seen her brush her hair, read a book, talk on the phone. I'd noticed that we had the same ballet poster hanging on our walls. I had never seen her pull down the shades, have friends over, or listen to records. Or. Or. Or . . .

Just last year, half the neighborhood had been emptied of those with special privileges, because a bunch of them turned out to be bona fide Soviet spies, caught in the act of stealing state secrets. But not our neighbors. They seemed to be the only ones who hadn't been deported. She was as Soviet and Communist as they come.

"Yrena," Todd said. "Isn't that a beautiful name? Like a poem?"

I had reached my limit. I punched Todd hard in the shoulder to snap him out of his stupor.

"Ow," he said.

"Put your eyes back in your skull," I told him. "You are setting back U.S.-Soviet relations fifty years with your tongue wagging around like that. You are going to cause Armageddon with your leering."

He ignored me.

"Okay. But, Rose, be honest. Do I look okay?"

I gave him the once-over. With his overgrown mutton-chops, he looked like a soulful sheepdog—not at all like someone who could cause any trouble.

But, I thought, he was also a sack of hormones. Todd was

skinny skin skin with a sunken chest. He wore wiry glasses like John Lennon's and his face was a little too shiny. But he didn't need to know that. He just needed to know that he was letting his adolescent boy hang out a little too much.

I kind of softened.

"You look like you always do," I said.

He seemed relieved, and I realized (at least a little) that my brother was a good guy—even when he said dumb things.

"Russian girls are hot," he said now. "James Bond agrees with me. Just watch *From Russia with Love*."

As the girl next door got to the bottom of her front steps, she noticed me and Todd, like she always did when we left our buildings at the same time. There had been many mornings that fall when we all walked out of our houses at exactly the same time. That particular day happened to be the one when everything fell right into place. At the time, I thought it was just a coincidence. But it wasn't.

Yrena never smiled at us. Or waved hello. But that day she caught my eye as she stopped to smooth her hair and check the pins in her bun, fixing the large white bow she always wore on top of her head.

Not for the first time, I wondered how good a dancer she was.

Is she better than me? I thought. Probably. No matter how badly I wanted to be good, it seemed like everyone was always a better dancer than I was.

I tried to push the dark thoughts out of my head. I wanted one part of me to be good today.

"Oh my God, is she looking over here?" Todd said. "Walk slower."

Todd slowed down his gait until he fell twelve paces behind me. I slowed down, too, but that made Todd walk even slower until finally I just stopped and waited for him to do what he needed to do to leer at Yrena as she passed us.

When she walked by me, she was looking at me and so maybe that's why I gave her the I'm-sorry-my-brother-is-a-perv look and she pressed her lips into a tiny smile that said to me It's-okay-and-I-understand-that-boys-will-be-boys.

Then we both smiled. For real. And I had to catch my breath because it was the friendliest moment I'd had in weeks.

I took that smile and I put it right where the hole in my chest was. It was better than coffee, or chocolate, or a perfect pirouette. I clutched it and held it tight.

"I seriously think I'm in love," Todd said as he watched Yrena retreat toward her school in the big white apartment building down the street.

"You are not in love," I said. "You don't even know her."

"I want to know her," Todd said.

"You will never know her," I said. But I think I said it sadly, because at the time I was thinking that I would never know her, either.

She was around the corner now and we could no longer see her. The KGB and the CIA guys had followed her,

7

presumably to make sure that she actually made it to the fenced-in white building.

"What do her parents do?" I asked Todd.

"I don't know," he said.

"How come you don't know that?"

I said it teasingly. Like he should know. But he took it to be a judgment. Todd was sensitive like that. Sensitive like me.

"I'm not that good a spy," Todd said, sounding genuinely disappointed in himself.

"They probably just work at the UN. Or maybe at the consulate," I said.

"Maybe they *are* spies. Maybe they're just so good that they didn't get caught in that sweep last year."

"You'd like that, wouldn't you?"

"Well, it would be *interesting.*"

My gaze floated over to the white apartment building. It was only when you noticed the large electric barbed wire fence patrolled by armed guards and a big Soviet flag flying from a flagpole that you began to see that it wasn't your average Riverdale apartment building.

I wondered if all the American flags that people on our street had waving in their yards were in response to that big red flag.

"Did you know that, technically, if I threw a ball over that fence, it would be in the Soviet Union?" Todd said. "With all the KGB and CIA, we probably have the safest street in New York City."

"Unless there's an international incident," I pointed out. "Then I guess we're screwed."

"I can think of lots of ways that maybe we could bridge the gap between the U.S. and the USSR. There could be a cultural exchange. We could have some kind of U.S.-USSR dating service. I could volunteer to date Yrena."

"What makes you think she'd want to go on a date with you?" I asked.

"I'm pretty brilliant," he said. Todd was not even kidding—he *was* brilliant. He had been smart enough to skip grades and go to college early, but instead he chose to stay with his age group and go to Bronx Science for a normal high school experience. I went to the High School of Performing Arts for dance.

"Probably I'd be a person of interest," he went on. "I could grow up to be almost anything."

I was glad that Todd and I didn't go to the same school, not only because Daisy, my ex–best friend, went to Bronx Science, but also because I didn't want to have to live up to Todd's academic reputation. When I was in junior high school, all the teachers expected me to be as smart as Todd, and then were inevitably disappointed when I barely hit average.

Still, Todd was uncoordinated, knock-kneed, ungraceful, and gangly. He couldn't even tap his foot in time while sitting down. I'd like to think that as smart as he was, there was a little part of him that was jealous of me for my dancing abilities, however flawed they were.

Todd and I walked in silence, each lost in our own early morning thoughts, till we got to the bottom of 254th Street and Broadway. Todd joined up with a group of Bronx Science kids and I stood off in my usual spot, off to the side and by myself.

No one I was friends with from junior high school went to Performing Arts, except for Stanley—but I hadn't talked to him since fourth grade, so he didn't count. Also, he was in the drama department and I especially didn't like the Drama (capital *D*, please) people. They thought they were all so cool, but really they were just *dramatic*. I thought they were too loud and wore too much makeup. Even Stanley.

High school sure had changed him.

I remembered when everyone gave Stanley the silent treatment in fourth grade. Or when he left a green turd in the bus toilet on the way to the dude ranch on the sixth-grade trip. Or when his too-tight, too-high pants split right in the crotch when he ran onto the stage for a chance to sing "Food, Glorious Food" from *Oliver!* in an assembly in eighth grade.

But now I noticed that, despite the fact that Stanley was the same old Stanley, he had a lot of friends, and his weird fashion sense looked kind of cool. He looked like he belonged.

I was still the same, and yet nothing had changed for me.

Of course, someone like Daisy would say that everything

about me had changed completely and that was why we could no longer be friends.

I tried not to notice her, but she was there at the bus stop, like she always was, hanging out with my old group of friends. We were far beyond the "hi" stage.

It used to be that, for a while, everyone except Daisy would smile at me when I got to the bus stop. Sometimes they would even ask me how I was, or how Performing Arts was. But in the last few weeks, that had all stopped. Daisy had made sure it had stopped.

Now they all left me alone, and when I got there, Daisy always looked at me and squinted her eyes into a hard stare.

Instead of being freaked out by her staring, I tried to notice how Daisy had changed. Her hair had more mousse in it than actual hair. It was shiny and her curls looked stiff. She wore big earrings that dangled in seemingly impossible geometric shapes. Even worse, she had on a miniskirt with leg warmers.

I hated it when nondancers wore leg warmers.

Daisy's black eyeliner made the mean look she was throwing at me even meaner. I felt that look right in my gut. I tried to look away, but I wasn't fast enough. I still saw what Daisy mouthed at me.

I hate you.

I could read her lips plain as day. No one else saw, and she didn't say it out loud. It was just for me.

I tried to remember to smile, like I was suddenly remembering something fantastic. Something funny. Something that I had to do. But I'm a dancer. Not an actress.

So instead, I think I cringed.

She must have seen me do it, because she laughed really loudly and turned back to her friends, leaving me with the same old cold shoulder.

She was the main reason that my heart was so dark. Why everything was black. We hadn't talked since summer. I couldn't help worrying that I had made the wrong choice and betrayed our friendship by choosing to dance.

I'm so stupid, I thought. *I'm not even that good.*

I had to stare at my shoes to focus myself. I bit the skin off around my fingers till they bled. It didn't really hurt. I was used to pain like that. My feet were a bloody mess from dancing.

I stepped farther away from the other kids and closer to the curb. Todd was too busy with his friends to notice. I was relieved and thankful when my bus came first so that I didn't have to be left standing at the bus stop all alone.

It felt better to be the first one to leave.

Notes from the Playground

The whole ride to school (first bus, then subway), I thought about what it meant to be someone's friend.

What was a friend? Really?

Someone you liked. Who was kindred. Who understood you. Who helped you. Who you had fun with. Who supported you. Who believed in you. Who accepted you. I realized that I'd never really had that with anyone. Not even Daisy. And now, every time I thought about being someone's friend, hers was the friendship that haunted me.

Deep down, had I known all along that we would come to such a bad end?

The first time I met her was in the second grade. At recess, we got into a fight over a swing at the playground. So I hit her with it. She had to have twelve stitches. The next day at recess, I was benched for my bad behavior and she wasn't allowed to play because of the stitches.

Sometimes, circumstance and incident are what make you

relate to one person and not another. Daisy and I started talking because we were stuck on the bench together.

"We both have flowers for names," Daisy said after a long stretch of playground watching. Watching people play when you wanted to play was very boring and terrible, so I was glad for the chance to talk. It was something to break the monotony of sitting still.

"Yes," I said. "That's true."

"We could have a secret club," she said. "Just you and me."

"Really?" This was interesting. I'd never been in a secret club.

"We'd be the only members because we have flower first names."

"What would we do in this club?" I asked.

"Oh, club things," Daisy replied.

"Like a password and a song?"

"Sure. And we could be best friends."

"Okay," I said. I'd never had a best friend.

"But you have to say you're sorry for making me bleed."

"I'm sorry," I said, a bit confused by her offer. I didn't know it could be settled so easily. The idea of having a best friend was bigger than anything.

"I might have a scar forever," she said solemnly. "And it would be your fault."

I hadn't thought about that.

"I'm *really* sorry," I said, and this time I actually meant it with all of my heart.

"And because you're sorry, that's why you'll have to do what I say," Daisy said. "And then we'll be best friends."

"Okay," I said.

Having a best friend was fun, even if I didn't like many of the things that Daisy liked. It was more important to just be her friend. I did whatever she said. I liked whatever she liked.

We had sleepovers all the time and we wore matching outfits to school. I got so good at thinking the same things were cool that people joked that they couldn't tell us apart. That we were like twins.

Our mothers signed us up for everything together, but our favorite thing was ballet. We were obsessed with going to the ballet, making up ballets, and having everything we owned be pink.

It was the only thing that we ever did together that I actually liked for real.

Everything was fine until sixth grade, when I was asked to go into the pre-pointe class and she wasn't.

"Ballet is stupid—we're quitting," Daisy announced. "We're in sixth grade now, so we're too old for it. Ballet is like dolls—it's something you grow out of."

And just like that, it was supposed to be over. But I hadn't grown out of it. I'd grown into it. It was my morning and evening. It was my breathing in and my breathing out. It was my food and my water.

I didn't want to quit. I couldn't. So I kept taking ballet.

At first I didn't tell her. I thought that she wouldn't

notice. I should have known right then that Daisy wasn't a real best friend. You don't lie to a best friend. You feel safe with her.

"Where were you?" she asked me one afternoon, a month into my attempted deception.

"Nowhere," I said.

"You're still going, aren't you?" she asked. "I can smell the tutu on you."

"I like ballet," I said.

"I'll never be your friend if you choose ballet over me."

I thought about it. I had to. Daisy was my best friend and I was betraying her. But *quitting ballet*? That seemed even more awful than losing Daisy.

I chose ballet.

That year, Daisy got the whole school to give *me* the silent treatment.

Almost every day after school, I took a bus downtown and took ballet. But in the end I wasn't convinced that it was worth the suffering that I endured at school every day. The silent treatment wore me down.

I hadn't made any other friends at ballet class over the years because Daisy and I had always been so inseparable, impenetrable. Nor was I the best in my pre-pointe class. I was close to the worst. The teacher kept telling me that my turn-out was bad, my extension was awful, and my arms were wobbly. And that I was lazy.

In sixth grade, I cried every night.

By the end of the year, I couldn't take it anymore. I quit.

Daisy immediately sniffed it out on me. It was easy to tell because one day after school, instead of leaving early with my big dance bag, I was just there, ready to hang out.

"I knew you'd see the light," she said. "Ballet is stupid. Friendship is much more important."

I stepped right back into being her number-one best friend, going along with whatever she said.

On the surface, everything was good. I was the perfect teenager. But underneath, I started having these moments where I would panic a little. Like maybe I was missing out on something bigger, more important, more beautiful.

Walking down the halls with my books in my hand, I would chassé. Sometimes outside while we all hung out, I would do a double pirouette. Occasionally when we had to run in gym class, I would throw in a leap or two. It seemed that no matter how much I tried to squash it, dancing always tried to gurgle up.

"What are you doing?" Daisy would ask.

It was only when Daisy spoke—and she spoke a lot—that the impulse to dance would stop.

"Nothing," I would tell her.

"It looked like dancing," she said.

"I was just goofing off."

"Well, you looked silly. Don't do it."

I swallowed it. Because I liked being the girl who got invited to parties and who could go to Johnson Avenue after school, go to Seton Park, and be available to *do stuff*. Outside, I was popular. Inside, I was aching.

This truce lasted until it was time to think about high school.

"What are we going to do about next year?" I asked as eighth grade advanced.

"Well, if I don't get into Bronx Science or Stuyvesant, then I'm going to private school," Daisy said.

No one wanted to go to a bad high school. Everyone knew you needed to get into one of the top high schools in the city or else you'd never go to one of the top colleges in the country.

"My parents aren't rich," I said. "They already told me that I'd just have to go to public school. We have to study really hard."

But Daisy didn't want to study *too* hard. Not when there were boys to chase, trends to set, and girls lower on the totem pole to make fun of.

I wasn't convinced that I could get into those brainy schools. I was smart, but I wasn't smart like Todd. I had a different kind of smarts, and that kind of smarts didn't do very well on tests.

The night before I took the high school placement test, I woke up at two in the morning and had a full-blown panic attack. What if I got all the math problems wrong? What if *amplifier:ear* was not the same as *telescope:eye*?

That's when it dawned on me, like *thunder:storm* or *wind:tornado*.

The thing I had going for me was *dance*.

School Sucks

The Van Cortlandt Park–242nd Street subway station was a terminus, so there was always a train waiting on the tracks. That day—the day I was destined to meet Yrena—I picked the car with the best-looking graffiti on it. It was a car covered in intricate letters that colorfully spelled out the words *Faith* and *Trust*.

I had my choice of any seat, but it felt weird to be the only person sitting in an empty car and be right in the middle of it, so I chose to sit in the corner.

As other kids from school boarded the train, I didn't bother nodding at them. They never sat with me even if they noticed me. Even if there was an empty seat next to me. Even if I tried smiling at them.

I was not friends with them. I was not friends with anyone. That's the trouble when you took everything black. You couldn't let any color in, either.

Maurice Tibbets got on at 86th Street. There was always a crowd around Maurice Tibbets. He had a lot of personality, and I knew from observation that he seemed to be fun to be around. And it couldn't have hurt that his mother was a superstar—Oscar-winning, Grammy-winning, Tony-winning Khadira. No last name necessary. Maurice was showbiz gold, and everyone at Performing Arts wanted to be near the glow.

I watched him on the sly as he hung on to the pole. Sometimes he'd let go and balance himself with his feet. He knew how to handle his body. Even on the moving train, he always knew where his center was. That's what made him the most talented dancer in freshman year.

I wished I was as talented as he was. Holding my back strong, I stood up and tried to find the center in my body. For a second I felt it, like a tiny golden ball inside of me that I could roll around gently. Then it disappeared, making me slouch again. But for a moment—a brief, certain moment—I had known what it felt like. For the rest of the trip I tried to get that feeling back.

At Times Square, we all got off in one big mass of pushing bodies. We were all going in the same direction, but still I trailed behind the others and their little cliques. There were the drama kids. There were the dancers. There were the musicians. There was the mixed group. I wanted to enter one of the little galaxies of friends, be one of the suns, even one that lived on the outermost arm, but I was too far-flung to be drawn in.

How did they find each other? I wondered. *How did they know that they could be friends?*

I had vowed that after what had happened with Daisy, I would take my time finding friends. I would go slowly. Now, two months into school, I still hadn't made a move, and everyone seemed to be all cliqued up.

I couldn't help but eavesdrop on the galaxies of friends while they laughed and talked about homework and the opposite sex and what was on TV last night. I walked through Times Square — eyes down, ears open — holding my breath because Times Square stank. I hated that I had to do this walk alone, past the marquees for *Dirty Sluts*, *Hot Cherry Girls*, *Madam o' Glam*. It was all porno theaters and dirty bums panhandling and prostitutes hanging around on the corners, even this early in the morning.

Every day, though, somehow I made it through. I had run the gauntlet by myself one more time. And despite how low I might have felt about my lot in life, whenever I saw everyone hanging out in front of the brown school building on 46th Street, I let out the breath that I had been holding in.

I made my way over to an empty spot off to the side of the building, away from everyone else, and began my morning of standing around, people watching. Some dancers on the corner had laid down a piece of cardboard on the sidewalk and were taking turns break dancing. I watched as they threaded the needle, went around the world, and practiced their freezes. Other kids surrounded the dancers, moving and clapping to the music coming out of a windowsill ghetto blaster. Early-rising tourists with cameras took pictures of the building and everyone who happened to be standing outside. I think they expected that we would start to dance on the taxicabs, just like in the movie *Fame*. The real cool kids gave the tourists the finger. I just tried to melt into the wall. I didn't want to be someone's souvenir.

"Rose!"

I heard my name and wondered if there was another girl at Performing Arts named Rose.

"Rose!"

I looked over and noticed Callisto and Caitlin, two triplets from my homeroom. They were waving someone over — waving *me* over.

"Rose!" Callisto called my name a third time and then patted the wall next to where she was leaning.

I pointed at my chest.

"Me?" I asked.

Callisto's head nodded up and down. I could have done a million things then. I could have shrugged. Or ignored them. Or gone into the building and up to the locker room to hide. But instead, that day, I picked up my bag from the ground, weaved my way through the break-dancers and the huddles of other kids, and went over to join them.

Callisto immediately offered me a clove cigarette from her fresh pack.

"Want one?" she asked.

"No," I said. My lungs were already filled with a dark smoldering discontent. I had enough smoke inside of me.

She shrugged and put one in her mouth and lit it up.

I liked the smell of clove cigarettes and found I didn't mind at all when Callisto blew the smoke right in my direction. It was a sweet smell, and its effect was calming, like incense. I leaned back against the wall and thought about Yrena's smile and my mother's warm hand and how nice it was to have someone to stand with that morning.

Today is going to be a good day, I thought.

"Are you staring at my earrings?" Callisto asked.

Callisto was very New Wave. She had her hair cut to look a lot like Ziggy Stardust. I knew this because she wore a denim jacket with a picture of Ziggy on the back that she got some guy down in the Village to paint for her. She wore three silver earrings in her left ear but none in her right one.

"I'm sorry," I said, blushing. Because I *had* been staring—not in a disapproving way, just in a fixing-my-gaze-on-something-while-thinking-deeply way.

"I always wanted to get a second hole, but my mom won't let me," I said.

"Our mom cried when Callisto came home with those extra earrings," Caitlin said. "She couldn't believe the lady at the mall would shoot extra holes in someone's ears without parental permission."

"She was worried that I looked too tough and would never be taken seriously as a concert violinist," Callisto said.

Caitlin, Callisto, and their triplet brother, Caleb, were all musicians, although Caleb was going to Performing Arts for drama, not music. He never stood with his sisters in the morning—in fact, I rarely saw him in front of the school. He had his own friends and they usually went to the parking lot across the street where the kids smoked who-knows-what.

Caitlin had shoulder-length wavy hair and wore liquid eyeliner, Cleopatra-style. Callisto looked nothing like her. You'd never know that they were sisters, or even triplets, except I had noticed that sometimes all three of them moved their hands the same way.

"Rose," Callisto said. "Important question. Did you study for the geometry test?"

"Not really," I said. I'd actually forgotten all about math class.

"Darn, me neither. I was hoping I could cheat off of you."

"Sorry."

I didn't know if I was supposed to move away from them after they were done talking to me or if I was supposed to stay. They didn't seem to mind me staying, so I stayed.

"Any plans for Halloween, Rose?" Caitlin asked.

"No plans," I said.

Out of the corner of my eye, I noticed Maurice and a bunch of other dance students stubbing out their cigarettes. They were all heading up to the locker room to change into their dance clothes because dance class was first period and they wanted to get there early to warm up.

I knew I should be doing the same, but I never did. Mostly it was because I hated being in the locker room while all the other dancers were talking and having fun. I wore my dance clothes underneath my street clothes and always ran in to change at the last minute.

That day, however, I didn't go up early because I was hanging out with Callisto and Caitlin and they were talking to me and there was no way that I was going to leave that spot, not even if the Soviet Union sent a nuclear missile to destroy New York City.

"Why are there no cute sophomore boys?" Callisto asked.

"I wish Elliot Waldman would come over and talk to me," Caitlin said. "He is such a dream."

I joined them in staring at Elliot Waldman and his friends, who were seniors, as they walked back toward the school from the parking lot across the street. Caleb and some other underclassmen were with them.

"Elliot Waldman is the only person at this school worth drooling over," Caitlin pronounced.

At exactly the same time, Caitlin and Callisto each put one hand on her forehead and one hand on her heart, as though they were fainting.

"What do you think, Rose? I bet you're the kind of girl who thinks David Freddy is hot."

It was a fact that most girls who went to the High School of Performing Arts were either in the Elliot Waldman camp or the David Freddy camp. Some girls thought that David

Freddy was the hottest thing since sliced bread. Personally, neither Elliot's leather jacket nor David's long hair did it for me.

My idea of hot was a perfect extension. My idea of hot was a guy looking good in tights. My idea of hot was the way that Maurice Tibbets balanced without the pole on the subway, even though I didn't like Maurice Tibbets like that.

The first bell rang, so I didn't have to answer Caitlin and Callisto. I just grabbed my bag and waved good-bye as I dashed into the building ahead of them.

"See you in homeroom!" Caitlin called after me as she joined the other music kids rushing inside to tune their instruments.

I raced upstairs to the dance department, peeled off my street clothes, and did a quick five-minute warm-up before Ms. Zina walked in with her limp and her cane and made us work up a sweat.

In dance class no one spoke. Everyone was completely concentrated. There was only the music, the instructions from Ms. Zina, and the shapes our movements made.

With the piano player tinkling away at the piano, and all of our feet making thumps and squeaks on the floor as we moved through the class, and the early morning sun streaming in through the windows, I felt as though I were in another world. Even though I always hung back a little, dance class was the only place that I felt good.

All of my feelings went right into my body.

I felt more like the real me when I danced — and that included the million little mistakes I made, which frustrated me. My arms felt floppy. My legs seemed weak. My extension was not high enough. My turn-out was terrible.

Why do I have to suck so much? I thought.

There were things that I could do to be better. I could show up early and warm up. I could ask questions about how I was supposed to make my body move like that. I could ask for help.

But I didn't.

By the time homeroom came around, which was right before third period, I was exhausted. Telling myself I wasn't good enough exhausted me.

I threw my street clothes on quickly and headed for homeroom. There, I could have a moment to lay my head down on the desk and shut my eyes while the homeroom teacher, Ms. Lana, took attendance.

"Here," I mumbled when she called my name.

"Hey, Rose," Caitlin said, poking me back into the world. "You wanna come over to our house this Sunday for Halloween? Our parents are out of town."

"We could go egg a house or do shaving-cream bombs," Callisto said.

I am a girl who loses friends, I thought. *I am a girl who can't keep friends.*

I wanted to avoid disappointment.

"It'll be so great," Callisto said.

Despite the big sign on the bulletin board that said INSTRUMENTS MUST REMAIN IN CASES DURING ACADEMIC CLASS AND HOMEROOM, Caitlin had pulled out her guitar and was now strumming quietly.

"No," I said. "I've got to be home."

Callisto shrugged. "I told you so, Cait," she said. "Well, how about pizza after school?"

"Say yes. Say yes. Say yes," Caitlin chimed in.

I found myself thinking: *When something is meant to be, it is just meant to be. You can put the brakes on as much as you want, but it will happen anyway.*

"Okay," I said, looking down at my nail-bitten hands. "I can do pizza after school."

It was as simple as that. Once you say yes, after saying no for so long, it becomes a lot easier.

Caitlin and Callisto high-fived.

"Don't flake on us," they said as the bell rang and they split up down the hallway.

There were some things that I admired about Callisto and Caitlin. Even though I was not in the music department, I had heard them play in the hallways, in homeroom, and at lunchtime. They were always game for an impromptu jam session or to accompany anyone who wanted to sing or dance.

They were very talented, like everyone here at school was, but they took their talent with such stride. They had this attitude, like, either they would be musicians or they wouldn't, and it was no big deal. Music was just one part of their lives.

I was not relaxed about dancing. I wished I could be sure that I was going to be a dancer for real. I wanted to be one so badly that the thought of not doing it or giving it up made me want to give up sunshine and dreaming and air.

I wasn't even near the best.

And that worried me. Only the best get to do what they want, right?

Only the *best*.

When I left school that afternoon, Callisto and Caitlin were there leaning against the building, waiting for me.

"Hey, let's go!" Callisto said, barely giving me a chance to say hello. "We've got to rush to get a good spot."

There were thousands of pizza places in New York City, but there was no doubt in my mind where we were going. Only one pizza place was cool enough for us Performing Arts students: Viva's. On my way home from school, I had often passed by and seen it so overstuffed with people that kids spilled out onto the sidewalk. The pizza always smelled so good and there was laughter as loud as the Spanish music that blared on the radio.

But I had never had the nerve to go in there by myself and order a slice for the trip back to the Bronx. I just clutched my bag tighter and walked by, trying to look like I had somewhere important to be, like a dance class or, even better, an audition.

Now here I was, walking through the doors with Caitlin and Callisto, and everyone was saying hello to them. To *us*.

Callisto managed to snag a table in the corner near Caleb, but he ignored her as he sat with the stoner drama kids, who languished there in leather jackets, army coats, and vintage sweaters, fine-tuning their broodiness.

We sat down with our sodas, waiting for the pie that was still cooking in the oven. I took my straw wrapper and blew the paper off, but instead of landing on the table, it flew off in the direction of the next table, hitting Caleb on the nose.

"Hey! What is your problem?" he yelled.

I shrank deeper into the corner.

He didn't think it was funny, but Caitlin and Callisto thought it was hysterical.

Caleb responded by crumpling up some greasy wax pizza paper and throwing it at our table. It hit Callisto in the worst possible place — her hair — and stuck there.

"Cool," Caitlin said. "It kind of looks like a small hat." She was obviously trying to soothe her sister from going ballistic.

"A pillbox hat," I chimed in, trying to help.

"Not my style," Callisto said.

Callisto plucked the wax paper from her hair. And then Caitlin shot me a look and motioned with her eyes. That's when I saw it — there was a string of cheese still hanging off of Callisto's hair, dangling all the way down to her ear.

Caleb and his tablemates erupted into howls of laughter.

"Looks like you've got a booger hanging off of your head," Caleb yelled over at her.

Caitlin reached over and carefully plucked the cheese off of Callisto's head, which messed up her hair.

"What are you doing?" she asked, irritated by the laughing.

Caitlin showed Callisto the cheese. Callisto shouted some curses and gave Caleb and his table the finger, which only made them laugh harder. But yelling had made her calmer, and so she spit into her hand and fixed her hair so that it was Ziggy-perfect again.

The crisis was over.

"I'm so glad you came out with us today," Caitlin said to me, putting her hand on my wrist.

Callisto nodded. "You're like one of the only people we can stand."

"But we know you're super shy," Caitlin added.

Caitlin and Callisto think I'm shy, I thought. *Maybe that's what I am.*

Shy.

"But you have so many friends at school," I said.

"Here comes one now," Caitlin murmured.

"But we don't really like her," Callisto said in an exaggerated whisper.

"Hey." A drama girl came over, interrupting us. She wore her hennaed curly hair down and long and was wearing a 1940s blue housedress. She had made her way over from a table that had a mix of dance and drama kids—the Broadway heads, not the angsty ones like Caleb. They were

32

the group that orbited around Maurice Tibbets and his famous-mother glow.

"Hello, Tammy," Callisto said.

"I thought I'd let you know that there is a party on the steps tonight."

Tammy's body had a vocabulary of nervous tics. For example, as she stood, I noticed that she would twist one of her hennaed curls and stick the tip of it in her mouth and suck on it. The edge of her hair was filled with sharp wet points.

"What steps?" I asked this out of curiosity, not out of a desire to go to a party. But it must have sounded that way. And maybe, deep down, I *did* want to go to a party. Maybe I was starving to go to a party. I hadn't been to a party since summer and that had been with Daisy and no fun at all.

"The Metropolitan Museum of Art," Tammy said, barely acknowledging my existence. "There's a scheduled impromptu party there every Friday night."

"How is it impromptu if it's scheduled?" I asked.

"It just is," Tammy said. "You should come. I've never seen you anywhere."

I tried to prevent this from upsetting me. But I had to blink a few extra times because my eyes sort of watered over.

"I don't know if it's my scene," I said, and I could hear myself trying to make it sound as though I definitely had a scene, and the reason why no one had ever seen me anywhere was because my scene was something else.

"Don't knock it till you try it," Tammy said, and then made her way back to the drama table, having delivered her message of partydom.

"Caleb!" Callisto yelled over to her brother. "Are you going to the party on the steps?"

"No way," Caleb said. "I only party on the rock."

"Good," Caitlin said. "We'll go if you go, Rose."

"Oh, I don't think so." I looked down at the table. "I wouldn't know anyone there."

"No one knows anyone there," Callisto said.

"That's why we should go together," Caitlin said.

"I don't think I can go," I insisted. "I don't like girls like Tammy. Those kinds of drama girls are so phony."

"Don't knock it till you try it," Callisto said, laughing.

"But you want to go, Rose. Deep down, I know you do. So just come," Caitlin said.

"No," I said. "I'm sorry. I can't."

"Well, I guess you can meet us there if you change your mind," Callisto said.

"Look at Tammy!" Caitlin elbowed Callisto and pointed. "She is *all over* Maurice."

I shot a look over to see Tammy hanging on to Maurice Tibbets, even as he attempted to eat a slice of pizza. She was draping her arms over his shoulders, and even though he kept shrugging her off and trying to lift the pizza to his mouth, her arms kept snaking back up around his neck.

"Starfucker," Callisto and Caitlin both said at the same time. And then they put their heads together and giggled.

"Did you know that Tammy smokes British cigarettes because she thinks that the UK is cool?" Caitlin said.

"She's so *affected*," Callisto said.

"Caleb does the best imitation of her. He says she's a nightmare in Graveson's drama class."

"She did her private moment in class the other day, and it was overdosing on pills. But wait, Caitlin—the UK *is* cool."

"I know, but Tammy doesn't like it for the right reasons," Caitlin said.

"Are there right reasons?" I asked.

This was my secret fear. That there were right reasons for liking things. That's why I usually just went along with whatever everyone else said.

"The British invasion of music," Callisto said. "David Bowie. Duh."

"Monty Python and Elfpunk. Stanley Kubrick. King Arthur!" Caitlin said.

"For anything on the BBC?" I offered. I wasn't sure. I was just asking.

"I knew it," Callisto said, putting her arm around my shoulders in a familiar way. "You *are* one of us."

Was that it? Was that the moment that everything changed? When Callisto said it, maybe something happened.

Maybe it was magic? Maybe it made me brave enough to put one step in front of the other. It was such a tiny thing.

"What do you think Tammy likes the UK for?" I asked.

"She likes it for Culture Club, *Chariots of Fire*, and Randy Prince Andy," Caitlin said.

Sometimes, you can't keep a laugh in. Even if you are just trying to be cool, to look cool. What Caitlin said made me laugh so hard that I nearly spit my Coke out of my nose.

"Oh, come meet us tonight, Rose," Callisto said. "I promise we'll have so much fun!"

My heart was fighting with my head. I wanted to say yes, but my head was so full of always saying no that only no could win.

"If I'm going to go to the Met, it's going to be to look at the art," I said.

"Oh, there will be art there," Callisto said. "The art of the party!"

By the time I had walked through my front door, I had convinced myself that I couldn't be friends with Callisto and Caitlin. It would be a bad idea. I decided that it was probably just best to put everything I had into something that I could control.

Plié. Tendu. Écarté. Chassé.

"There is pasta, or you can order Chinese—I left you twenty dollars," my mom called out to me from her bedroom. She was getting ready for a date night with my dad.

"I had pizza after school," I said. I came into her room and sat on the edge of the bed. "I'm not that hungry."

"Did you go out with some friends?" she asked. "You know, you can invite friends over."

I watched her as she stood in front of her full-length mirror wearing a smart pantsuit, sliding her big loop earrings in her ears.

She went on. "I just hate to think of you here by yourself,

Rose. It's not natural for a healthy teenage girl like you to spend so much time alone."

"I'm not really alone. Todd has his Dungeons and Dragons game down in the garage," I said.

She gave me a look through the mirror that said she wasn't buying what I was selling.

"I just think that you are by yourself too much." She turned around and faced me. "I want to meet some of your friends," she said slowly. She said it as though she had practiced saying it. As though she had read it in a book called something like *How to Deal with Your Angsty Teenager*.

She was *fishing*.

I didn't want to answer her because she wasn't asking me a question.

She stood there looking at me, giving me the time I needed to say something. *Anything.*

I had no words. I only had movement. If I could have gotten up and showed her with my body, with my movements, how I felt, would she understand? Would she feel better about what I was saying?

My mother was staring at me. And then I remembered the way she had cupped my face that morning.

I opened my mouth.

"Well, I had pizza after school with Callisto and Caitlin," I said. "They're triplets. I mean, two out of the three. They're in the music department. They don't look alike. At all. Weird, huh?"

She seemed relieved. Then she came over to the bed and gave me a little love pinch before going back to her primping.

After my parents left for the evening and Todd headed downstairs to prep his D&D game, I brought my ghetto blaster into the bathroom and slipped in a mix tape. ("Tainted Love," "Stop Draggin' My Heart Around," "Every Little Thing She Does Is Magic," "We Got the Beat," "Girls on Film," "I Know What Boys Like," "Shake It Up," "Open Arms," "Centerfold," "I Love Rock-n-Roll," "The Tide Is High," "Kids in America.")

I drew a hot bath and filled it with Epsom salts. I lit some candles. I filled the tub up high so that the water went right up to my chin.

This was my favorite thing to do on Fridays, soak in a long, hot bath. I needed the hot bath and the salts because my muscles were always sore from dancing all week.

First I would slip my bloody blistered feet into the tub. It stung a bit at first, and the bath was always a little too hot initially, but I knew it was going to feel good.

Then I would sink down into the water, letting it cover me completely. I felt all the bones in my body. I rubbed all the muscles. I closed my eyes. I stretched and released.

My body played out that week's classes. That week's combinations. That week's mistakes. In the tub, when I closed my eyes, I could imagine standing half a chance at doing the combinations perfectly.

Relaxed, I got out of the tub and went into my room where I pulled on snowflake-patterned long underwear and an antique pink slip from the 1940s that belonged to my Grandma. It was cold, so I put leg warmers on my arms. I wasn't making a fashion statement.

I had just taken my hair out of the towel and was about to brush it, but was distracted by a zit that was forming on the end of my nose. (Later my hair looked good because of the way that it had dried, in a way that I could have never planned. Another happy accident.)

I wasn't paying attention to anything else but my extreme close-up, and this one little clogged pore, which magnified by one thousand looked totally gross. Pores were totally gross. That's what I was thinking when something hit my bedroom window.

"Ahhhhhhhhhhhhhh!" I yelled.

Even though it was probably a branch or the wind, my immediate thought was: *It's a pervert. On the fire escape.* There were perverts in the Bronx. I knew this to be true because my brother, Todd, was a pervert and he lived in Riverdale. I also knew that his dorky friends were perverts, and they were all downstairs in the garage playing Dungeons and Dragons. Right now, my house was Pervert Central.

Maybe it was one of Todd's friends pulling a Peeping Tom on me at the window. They all knew I was here alone upstairs and they had such limited contact with girls that they would do anything to see me in my underwear. Todd had probably

40

told them that I was bathing. I grabbed a sweater. I wanted to cover myself up. I put it on backward to have maximum coverage over my chest area. (I might not have had big boobs, but to most boys, boobs are boobs.)

The noise at the window became more insistent and I started to really freak out.

Maybe, I thought, *it's a killer.*

Things like that had been known to happen. There could have been a killer at the window.

I didn't want to turn toward the window because I was afraid of what I might see. I was totally spinning out and having a massive panic attack. I wanted to sneak out of my room, but I knew whoever was there could see me because all of my lights were on. So I started to edge my way over to the door, kind of wishing that I wasn't such a slob because if I wasn't a slob, then the floor would be clear and I would have an easy path to the door and out of the room, and then instead of it taking me what seemed like hours to inch out of my room, I'd be far away from the horrible thing at my window as quickly as possible.

Then there was a voice.

"Hello?"

A girl's voice.

With a Russian accent.

Definitely not a pervert, a friend of my brother's, or a murderer.

"Hello?" the voice said again. "It's Yrena, your neighbor."

I turned around and looked and, sure enough, there was Yrena, pressing her face up to my window. I barely knew her to say hello when we passed each other on the street, so I didn't really know why she had shinnied up to my window.

I wasn't scared anymore. Instead, I was mad that she had scared me.

I walked over to the window. Her face was goofier up close than it was when I saw her from afar. Or maybe it was just distorted by the glass. I opened the window and she fell into the room.

I ripped right into her. "Freaking a girl out is not the way to be neighborly. You could have been a murderer! Next time just ring the doorbell."

She smiled as she gave me her hands so I could pull her up. Which I did.

"Yrena," she said, smiling at me face-to-face now. She was a little bit taller than me. Her long blond hair was up in a tight bun, like always.

"Rose," I said.

"Rose," she said. "Like a flower."

For two years, she'd been on my radar, but I never took much notice. She was just there, doing her thing in my peripheral vision. Every now and then, though, she'd emerge and I'd pay attention. Those moments of hers that I'd notice were never big. It was just small things: doing her homework at night at her big brown desk, folding clothes and putting them in drawers, taking those white bows out of her hair, getting up to turn off the lights but always leaving one light on.

I noticed that she was wearing pants instead of a skirt. That was something new. I had never once, in the two years she lived next door to me, seen her wear pants.

As a dancer, I always sized up everyone's legs, and she had good, long legs. I would've killed for legs like that.

I imagined her dancing the combinations that we'd had in class that week. I imagined her getting through them flawlessly. She looked like a star.

"I've always wondered about your room," she said. "I can only see a part of it, you know. The rest of it is exactly how I thought it would be. It's so *American girl*."

Sometimes, when you don't know someone except for what you've gleaned through a bedroom window, you get a distorted view of what they are like. Yrena thought that I was a typical American girl, but the truth was that there was no such thing as a typical American girl. I was very typical for myself, but that was it.

I couldn't tell from her accent if her thinking that my room was so American girl was a compliment or a dis. I suspected it to be a dis. I didn't need to be dissed in my own room. Not when I had just been scared that she might be a pervert.

"What does that even mean?" I asked.

"You have many things that you don't need," she said.

Then she went over to my vanity and fingered the new pair of Freed of London pointe shoes I had lying there because I had to break them in.

Then she went to the wall, where she gently handled the pointe shoes that I had tacked on there. Those were the special ones, signed by dancers I admired: Natalia Makarova, Suzanne Farrell, and Gelsey Kirkland. I had gotten them after shows that I had seen when I was a little girl. It was a dorky thing to do, maybe, but those dancers were my heroes and those shoes had touched the stage that I wanted to dance on.

She moved on to the wicker basket on the floor where I kept every single pair of pointe shoes I'd ever had. Most of the shoes were trashed, but I couldn't seem to throw them away. She picked through them, turning each shoe over to examine the stitching, the shanks, the bend, the wear. It made me self-conscious, like she was reading my fortune. If she looked too closely, she'd know everything there was to know about me. That I wanted to shine, but I didn't.

"Why are you going through my stuff?" I asked.

"Your right leg is stronger than your left. I am the opposite," she said. Her English was not bad, and her accent made her say things in a charming singsong way.

Right then, something switched. It went from her picking through the things in my room as though it were the most natural thing in the world to this dancer shorthand. Something about Yrena standing there seemed familiar. Maybe it was something about dancers when they got together. I watched as she looked around the room like she wanted to do some dance moves to demonstrate her weak leg, but there was no space on the floor on account of my room being a pigsty.

She gave up trying to show me and came over to the bed and plopped down very gracefully next to me, like Odile dying in *Swan Lake*. Then she put her arms around me and gave me a quick embrace.

A hug, from someone who appreciated the things in my room. She looked at me and stuck her tongue out and crossed her eyes, and for some reason that just about made my heart crack open.

I didn't know her at all, and even though she had broken into my room, nosed through all of my stuff, and was acting like we were bosom buddies for no good reason, I liked her.

"This is so fun!" she said. "To finally be in your room! To finally speak with you!"

I didn't know what kind of fun I was supposed to be having in this situation. Maybe a little bit like how I felt at Viva's with Caitlin and Callisto. It was confusing to suddenly be saying hello to my next-door neighbor for the first time, even though it didn't feel like the first time. It was confusing to suddenly act like we'd really known each other for the past two years when we most definitely had not.

I wondered what Yrena wanted.

"What do you want?" I said, trying not to sound rude, because I wasn't trying to be. I was trying to be open, because she was so open. Her face, her spirit, her excitement, were so open. It was infectious. She was sitting there on my bed, almost bouncing up and down, like a little kid.

I started to bounce, too. With anticipation. We both started to giggle. When you giggle, it's different from laughing. Giggling is like bubbles that lift you up, no matter how hard or dark your spirit is.

"I have always wanted to come into your room," she said. "It has been a great mystery to me since I moved here. I have often seen you in your room through your window and wondered about you."

I understood what she meant completely. She wasn't judging me — it was just like she said, she was genuinely interested. I was a *great mystery*.

"You never close your curtains," I said. "I always close my curtains because of the streetlamp. Doesn't it shine into your room, too?"

I never saw her curtains closed, not even when I came home late at night. It was weird. And she always seemed to have a light on.

"Are you afraid of the dark?" I asked. I had often wondered if maybe she was afraid of the dark.

"No," Yrena said. "I like to always be able to look outside."

"But there's not much to see outside," I said.

She threw her hands up in the air.

"There are a million things to see!"

"Like what?"

46

Yrena stood up and pulled me over to my window.

"Birds! People! Clouds! Life!"

She was waving her arms around at everything. And when she said it, it sounded exciting.

"Do you know that you are the closest I've ever had to having an American friend?" Yrena said. "I mean to say, I always thought that we could be friends, even though you are American."

Then she put her hand over her mouth and kind of slapped her lips.

"I don't mean that we can't be friends because you are American!"

"I didn't think you meant that," I said.

"I am not like my father! My father would say that." Yrena looked genuinely mad at herself for this.

"It's silly," I told her. "Don't worry."

I didn't want her to worry. I didn't want her to feel bad. I didn't want her to be embarrassed.

I wanted to know more.

"Honestly, I never even knew that you spoke English."

"I do speak English. I have watched American television! It is a good skill to have. I speak French and Italian, too."

I would have to remember to mention that to Todd. He'd be stoked to know that he got something right, and to learn something new about Yrena.

She smiled at me. She had a gap between her two front teeth, and even though she was smiling, there was a kind of sadness about her that felt familiar to me. Her sadness seemed wistful. Nostalgic. Fragile. Like what I liked most about a beautiful performance. Something delicate and intensely human.

My sadness tended to repel, to alienate, to isolate. I tried to smile brighter.

It was nice to have someone sitting next to me to talk to.

I sighed.

She sighed back.

I didn't want her to have to go home. I looked toward the door because I could hear the garage opening and closing, which meant that either another of Todd's friends or the pizza had arrived. Yrena stood up and looked apologetic.

"You must want me to go so that you can go to the party," she said.

"The party?"

And then, just because I did have a party I could go to, and I wanted Yrena to think I was cool, I said, in a kind of big, kind of braggy voice, "I'm going to meet my friends Callisto and Caitlin at a huge party downtown. You should come with me."

I didn't know why I said it, except that it felt good to say it. It felt good to invite her. Thrilling. Daring. Out of control. My pulse quickened, like when I had to do the combination in class by myself, with all of those eyes staring at me. I got nervous. So nervous.

To calm myself a bit, I started getting ready, as if I really was going to go to the party and Yrena was really coming with me. She followed me around my room as I gathered things up. I put on my shoes. I put on a little makeup. But just before I started brushing my hair, Yrena spoke.

"Oh. I can't do that," she said.

"Oh. I see," I said.

Rejected. Raw. That little spark that I had felt had tricked me into stepping out, but I had been slapped back into place. I was disappointed. I hardened. Something had changed between us. I had misread the cues. I had gone left instead of right.

I put the brush down.

"I thought you would go to the party that happens every Friday in your garage," Yrena said.

"What party?"

"I thought maybe since it was just downstairs, that I could go there with you," she said sincerely.

"I think you've made a mistake. There is no party at my house."

When I looked up at her I could see that she looked sorry. Vulnerable.

"Sometimes, I am at my window and I see the boys going into the garage. And sometimes there is pizza. It looks like a big American party. I have always wanted to go. To be invited."

She was talking about my brother's D&D game, which was about as much of a rager as a mid-afternoon grandpa nap. I realized that it *could* be hugely misinterpreted as a party, if you didn't know all the facts. I felt a weight lift off of me. She wasn't rejecting me. She just couldn't leave the Bronx.

"That's not a party!" I told her. "My brother has his Dungeons and Dragons night every Friday. Trust me, you don't want to go there."

"Dungeons and Dragons?" Yrena asked, in a way that made it clear that geeky role-playing games with multi-sided dice hadn't yet made it to Moscow.

"It's a game where you pretend that you are a wizard or a fighter or something and you battle orcs and hunt for treasure and play with dice," I tried to explain.

"A game party?" She actually looked kind of impressed and interested. "My parents and I play card games together. It is fun!"

"Dungeons and Dragons is not cool," I said.

"Oh," she said, looking a bit disappointed. "I don't know what is cool or not cool."

That floored me. I would never admit that I didn't know what was cool or not. That kind of truth could only lead to more humiliation and alienation. I felt protective of Yrena; someone needed to show her how to be a teenager in America, or she would never survive. I knew I was barely surviving myself, but at least I had observed what to do. How to *be*. I would never consider myself an expert of cool. I didn't have my own opinions; I was never sure of them. In the past, when we were friends, I had always followed whatever Daisy said. And now I just listened to what everyone around me said was cool at school and tried to keep up. It was funny how some people just seemed to know what was cool and what wasn't. I definitely wasn't cool. But somehow, at that moment, I was the expert in the room.

"Dungeons and Dragons: not cool," I said again. Of that, at least, I was certain. I knew Todd would turn my life into one of his beloved slasher movies if he ever learned that Yrena had wanted to party with him and that I had convinced her not to be trapped in his nerd lair. There was just no way I was going to introduce Yrena to the role-playing rivals.

"So, there is not a party there every weekend?"

"It is definitely not a party," I said.

"I always thought that your brother's Friday parties were proof of teenage American decadence! I always wondered what it was like."

She said "teenage American decadence" with great joy, not like it was a bad thing. Like it was something that her parents said all the time to warn her.

"Well, I'm sure they wish it was," I said. "But it is most definitely proof of teenage American *loserdom*."

Yrena looked down at her jeans and started picking on a stray thread. She was doing that thing that I knew I had done a million times, where you tried to readjust your thoughts when you realized that everything you had previously thought about something was totally wrong.

She had probably written up a whole story in her head about me and my brother. She had probably thought she was being daring hanging out with me in my bedroom and asking to go to the party downstairs.

And what had I done? I had burst her bubble. I had let her down.

What did Yrena want? She just wanted something to do. I could come up with something to do.

"Do you like ice cream?" I asked.

"Yes," she said. "Who doesn't?"

"We could go up the street to Zips and get an ice cream."

"Okay."

I went to open my bedroom door, but Yrena whistled to me and motioned to the window and started to climb through it, disappearing outside.

I didn't stop to think about it. I didn't think it was weird. I just followed her out the window in my pink slip and backward sweater.

It was a funny thing, climbing out of a bedroom window. It got you out of the house, just like a door did, but somehow it made you look at your own house differently, as though the use of the window had just expanded into something more profound.

A window could be an exit.

Audition

I had two states of being. When I was on pointe and when I was in sneakers.

When I was on pointe, the world was heightened. I had a voice. I was really me.

And when I was in sneakers, I was nothing. I was a mouse.

I didn't want to be a mouse forever.

This was why, as eighth grade drew to a close, I'd booked myself an audition at the High School of Performing Arts. I dusted off my ballet shoes and cobbled together an audition piece using parts from an old recital I had done when I was twelve. I bribed Todd with homemade chocolate chip cookies for time in the garage to practice my moves.

I did it in secret. I didn't tell anybody what I was doing. Not even my parents. I did it like I was ashamed. Like if I told anyone—especially Daisy—I would be convinced to quit.

What was I thinking? That I could be a dancer?

Yes.

When I got to the school, the building looked ominous. It was nestled on the street just up the road from Times Square, which was a scary mess. I found myself in front of an old, run-down brown building.

I made my way upstairs to the dance department. I saw Stanley, from school, but he was auditioning for the drama department and the music department, so I didn't say hello. I knew he wouldn't rat me out to my friends because he didn't mingle in Daisy's circle.

I pinned the number that the audition check-in girl handed me onto my bodysuit and sat on the floor in my tights, stretching out against the mirror as I watched the other dancers in my group auditioning. They were good. They looked good. They looked cool. They looked skinny. I was woefully out of shape, my muscles tighter than they used to be. I stretched a little harder, but I didn't want to overdo it.

But even though I had quit dancing, even though my dancing was going to be rusty, at that moment I felt like a dancer.

I knew it the way that a bird knows how to fly when it is pushed out of its nest. The way that a baby penguin knows how to swim. How a flower knows to bloom in spring.

"Numbers five through ten, please take center," the woman with the accent and the cane yelled. She was small and hunched and her hair was shockingly short and white.

I was number nine, so I got up and took a place on the floor in the back row.

But suddenly, I didn't want to be seen, even if I was going to give it my best. Suddenly I felt *shy*.

The woman showed us the combination and we learned it quickly and did it. I thought perhaps we'd sit down like the other group had after they'd done it once all the way through.

But no. "This group again. And this time, let us have the two reluctant young ladies in the back do it in the front," the woman said, banging her cane on the floor.

(Later, I would learn that she limped because two of her toes were cut off, but at this moment I had forgotten why it always seemed as though ballet teachers were old as time and strangely misshapen.)

I moved to the front row. The piano player started to play, and I danced.

I was terrible. I stumbled. I missed a step, and even though I was still doing the combination, I figured I'd failed the audition already. I stopped trying. I knew what my fate was. It was the zoned school for me.

Everyone in the room could see that I was not up to par. I could feel my heart, and how much I wanted it to go into my feet. But my heart wouldn't comply. I was scared. My heart was pulling away from me rather than going where it was supposed to.

I danced as though disconnected. And the harder I tried to reach for it, the farther it went away from me. My fear had won.

When they called numbers to stay behind, my number

wasn't called. I knew that meant that I could go home. I knew that meant that I hadn't gotten a callback.

"Wasn't that so fun!" a girl next to me said as she put on her street clothes. "I hope I get in. This is my dream school!"

I knew for sure that she wasn't going to get in, because I had watched her and she was a bad dancer. I knew I wasn't *that* bad. I could blame my rejection on being rusty, out of shape, and mediocre at the audition.

But I couldn't absolve myself of the fact that none of this mattered, if you danced with no spark. If you kept something to yourself. That was probably worse than being bad.

That girl was lucky. It was better to be like her and to just have no talent at all than to have just a little bit of talent and not be able to even let it out.

I barraged myself. Maybe if I had practiced more in the garage . . . Maybe if I'd taken a few dance classes after school to help me get my dance back on . . . Maybe if I'd used different music in my solo piece . . .

There I was in the locker room, changing into my street clothes, when it hit me for real that I had totally blown it. I wanted to go to Performing Arts. Not a zoned school, and definitely not Bronx Science. I didn't want four more years of all of those people.

I slammed the locker shut with my hand. It popped back open and hit me in the forehead.

I was alone then, in the back corner so none of the other girls who had auditioned with me could see. Some of them must have been upset, too. Or maybe they didn't realize that they had been cut yet. I could tell they had some hope they were clinging to that they were going to get in because a few of them were chattering as they left the dressing room, like excited birds. They would go home and wonder and wait for their letter and be surprised or bummed out when it was a rejection.

I waited a bit until they had left and then I started crying. I didn't want anyone to see that I was upset. There were mirrors everywhere and I caught sight of myself, and was amazed because I didn't recognize myself.

Where had the real me gone? There I was, crying, in secret, dressed in street clothes that Daisy had made me buy at the Galleria. Why was I wearing this Fiorucci sweatshirt? I didn't even like it.

Seeing myself in all of those mirrors, so sad and in an outfit that I didn't like, that wasn't even me, made it more upsetting, so I pulled my sweatshirt up over my face so I couldn't see anything at all.

I waited until the whole locker room was silent and then I went out in the hallway.

I stopped to look at the bulletin board with pictures of the dance department that I would never be in.

That was when I saw her coming toward me, holding a sandwich bag under her arm and a to-go coffee cup in her hand—the woman with the limp who had auditioned me.

"You. Didn't I cut you an hour ago?" she asked.

I felt embarrassed.

I nodded.

"Why aren't you gone yet? There is no loitering."

I shrugged. I didn't want to speak in case I started crying again. I couldn't look at her face because it was so severe. She was all pointy angles, high forehead, purple lipstick, and that shock of extremely short, extremely white hair.

"You are out of shape, and you haven't danced in a long time, I think," she said.

I shook my head from side to side. No. I hadn't.

"You do not want to leave now, but you should have not wanted to leave when you were auditioning."

I nodded in agreement, because she was right.

"Do you remember the combination?" she asked.

"Yes," I said.

"Ah, she speaks," the woman said to the empty hall, as though there were a large audience around her and she was onstage. "Do it for me now."

"Here?" I said.

"Yes. Here."

"I'm not dressed right," I said.

"Does that matter? No. It does not. I asked you to dance for me. Dance does not care about clothes."

I put down my shoulder bag and took off my jacket and put them on the floor under the bulletin board. And then I did the combination. I channeled all my anger, all my disappointment, all of my simmering into the combination. I attacked it.

No errors. Not bad. Not great. But not bad. Definitely better than in the audition room.

"Do you feel better now?"

I nodded. I did feel better.

"Sometimes a combination is best remembered a little bit after it is learned."

"Muscle memory," I said.

She nodded.

"Watch your back leg—you tend to drag it and you are very out of shape," she said. And then she turned and retreated down the hallway.

When my letter arrived, I figured it was too thin to be an acceptance letter. I figured I must have been rejected.

But when I opened it, I had gotten in.

The first thing I did was take dance classes to get back into shape.

The second thing I did was try to figure out how I was going to tell Daisy that I was going to be a dancer.

You'd think that telling someone the truth would be easy. But it was harder than I thought, because I had quit dancing. Forever quit. Never-going-back quit. Totally-swore-up-and-down quit.

I got in to Science, too, but I knew there was no way that I was going to go.

Daisy was so excited.

"We're going to go down to Canal Street and get cool clothes. We're going to henna our hair. We're going to get ourselves summer boyfriends at the Mockridge pool for *practice*."

She had big plans for us at Science. She kept saying how we were going to reinvent ourselves over the summer and be the coolest freshman girls when we got there.

I let Daisy go on about our reinvention all summer. I went down to Canal Street and bought more things I didn't like. I wore my matching swimsuit to the Mockridge pool and pretended to have a crush on Danny Wasserman.

I waited until two weeks before school started to tell her. And even then it wasn't planned. I was at her house, sleeping over. She had gotten a letter telling her what homeroom she was in and she wanted to know if we were going to be together.

"I'm not going to Science," I said.

"What?" Daisy said. She was putting on purple eye shadow even though we weren't planning on going anywhere. It was a thing we did, experiment with crazy makeup when we had sleepovers. It was another thing that I didn't like to do. Daisy would bring over piles of magazines and her hand was guided by the New Wave look she found in them. She wanted to cultivate a style for high school.

"I thought you got in? I saw your acceptance!"

"I did get in," I said. "But I'm not going."

"We have a plan," she said. The shadow made her eyes look bruised. "We have to stick together. Just tell your parents you won't go to private school."

I sucked in my cheeks and started applying makeup, too.

"I'm not going to private school. I'm going to Performing Arts."

"What?" Daisy said, holding her blush brush midair. She only had one cheek done. "You can't just decide to go there. You have to *audition* to get in. Besides, you know who is going there? Stanley. And he's gross. Gross people go there."

It was ironic how she said she was all about the strange and different. That's what she liked best in the magazines. But there it was something contained and frozen on the pages, in its assigned role of the weird. It couldn't get loose and do something unexpected. She obviously couldn't stand someone in real life going off script.

"I auditioned and I got in."

"But you didn't tell me," she said.

"No, I didn't."

"But you tell me everything," she said. "Best friends don't keep secrets."

"Well, I'm sorry. I was afraid to tell you."

She stopped looking at me and only looked at her own image in the mirror. She resumed making herself up.

"Why?" she said slowly.

"I thought you'd laugh at me."

"Well, what talent do you have?" she asked, and to make it worse, now she was laughing, like she didn't know.

"Dance."

Daisy's eyes narrowed. Her cheeks were hot-pink triangles. She looked sharp and geometric.

"You know what your problem is?" she said. "You're a liar."

She threw the makeup brush at the mirror, snatched her bag off the floor, and pushed past me.

I grabbed her arm. "Where are you going?" I asked. "Just because we're not going to the same school doesn't mean that we can't be friends."

I wondered if I looked as surreal as she did, with wild-colored spots on my face, or if it was just the scene that she was making that made everything look absurd.

"Friends don't betray friends like that," she said, shaking me off. "We had a plan."

"I didn't betray you," I said. "I just made a different choice than what you wanted."

"We had a deal," she said.

And right at that moment, I wavered. My resolve broke. My knees were weak.

"Maybe I could change my plans," I said. "Maybe I can just go to Bronx Science."

"No," she said. "It's too late. I can never trust you again. You've ruined everything, and I will never be your friend again."

"Please," I said. "Please."

I begged her all the way down the stairs. All the way to the front door. All the way to the corner.

And then she turned around and spit at me so I would stop following her.

And that was the moment when I thought that maybe I shouldn't have any friends at all.

East Meets West

It was dark outside, so I didn't notice them until we got to the crosswalk on Mosholu Avenue. They walked under the streetlamp. Two men. They both had suits on. One was in front, the other trailing behind, both of them following us, but not together.

"KGB or CIA?" I said automatically to Yrena, like I always did to Todd.

She looked over her shoulder at them.

"You can tell by their shoes," she said.

I looked at the men's shoes.

"The black ones, KGB. The sneakers, CIA," I said.

"Yes, I think so, too," she said. "They are not interested in you. It's normal for them to follow us. It is not a big deal."

"Is that why you climbed through my window? To evade them?"

"I thought perhaps we had escaped them by going through the window," she said. "It's fun to try to escape them."

"Will we get in trouble?" I asked. I wasn't too worried. More curious than anything else.

"Only if we share state secrets," she said.

"Well, it's best to take the price tag off the bottom of a toe shoe," I said. "Otherwise, when you perform, it's distracting."

"That's it," Yrena said, throwing her arms up in the air. "We're certainly on a watch list now."

"What a drag," I said.

Then we laughed. Because at the time it was funny. I mean, what would two girls like us ever be on a watch list for? Exchanging microfilm in our sugar cones?

When we got to Zips, I ordered a mint chocolate chip ice cream sundae and Yrena ordered a strawberry one.

"What is your high school like?" Yrena asked. "Do you have a boyfriend? Is there a football team? Do your parents let you wear makeup?"

"I go to a special school," I said. "A school for performing arts."

"For dance?" Yrena asked.

"Yeah," I said. "So it's not like a regular American high school. We don't have gym class."

"No cheerleaders?" Yrena seemed saddened by this.

"No," I said. "Dance class, academics, and the occasional hot lunch."

"I was hoping you could tell me about cheerleaders. And football."

"I don't know anything about that. We don't have anything like they do in a normal high school. I mean, I guess maybe I'm missing out on a regular high school experience."

"Will you feel strange later on in life?"

"I don't think so," I said. "I think I'm kind of glad. Besides, isn't every school a bit different?"

Yrena shrugged.

"Well. At least we have a senior prom."

"That's a dance," Yrena said.

"Yes."

"We have dances. Although they try to keep it the same, my school here in America is different than back home."

"So I guess every school is different and the same."

"Yes," she said.

I thought about that for a minute. It was comforting to know that you could always find something in common with someone else.

"How long have you been dancing?" I asked.

"I took ballet class because all little girls take ballet," Yrena said flatly.

"Do you have a boyfriend?" I asked.

"I do not have a boyfriend." Yrena sighed. "My father says I am too young to go on dates." She took a spoonful of her ice cream and sucked on the spoon thoughtfully. "I will tell you a secret. I am hoping that because my breasts have grown so much—they are really quite big—that they will not take me back at the ballet school."

"Really?" I said.

"Yes," she said.

"You have some of the best schools in the world."

"How long have *you* been dancing?" she asked.

"Since I was four."

"Me, since I was three. But I do not want to dance. I want to quit."

"I thought for you Russians, dancing was in your DNA."

"I thought for you Americans, every girl was a cheerleader in love with a football player."

Sometimes it takes someone saying something stupid to make you realize that what you said was stupid.

"I quit dancing once," I said. "But it didn't stick."

"You are lucky," Yrena said. "My ballet master says that if you want to know if you are really a dancer, you should try quitting. If you can't, then you are a dancer."

"I didn't want to quit because I hated dancing. I quit because I just wanted to fit in more than I wanted to dance."

Yrena reached across the table, took my hand in hers, and squeezed it, as though she wanted me to know how much she understood what I was saying. It felt good to be so completely understood, so completely trusted.

"I want to be a normal girl," she said. "Do normal things. Not be special. Just a normal Russian teenager."

It was true—Yrena didn't seem typical. She was living in America, climbing into people's windows, wanting to go to

Todd's D&D party. I wondered what a normal Russian teenager looked like, because it didn't seem like one was sitting in front of me, any more than a typical American girl was sitting in front of her.

I went back to the question: *Aren't we all different and the same?*

"I told myself that I was over ballet," I said. "Not serious about it anymore. Tired of the endless repetition."

"Tired of the discipline," Yrena said.

"Tired of the aching muscles."

"Of the broken toes. The swollen feet."

We both said it. And in a way, despite our being from different places, Yrena kind of got it.

But I couldn't tell how Yrena felt about dancing. She seemed to love dancing as much as I did. But she seemed to hate it more than I did, too.

It was funny how two such different things could be true at the same time. I was tired of those things.

"I told myself all that and it made it easier to quit, and when I did, I had friends," I said.

"I don't have many friends since we moved to America," Yrena said.

She said it kind of matter-of-factly. And I thought about it, and how it must be hard for her, only having the other Soviets that were here in New York to socialize with. Just enough to fill an apartment building. I could barely find anyone to fit in with at school, and that was a building full of kids.

I brought the subject back to dance.

"I don't think I'm very good. There is always someone better than me in dance class," I said.

"There is always someone better," Yrena said. "Anywhere."

I wondered if I was better than anyone in class. From the way Ms. Zina barked at me, it didn't seem possible.

"I am always so relieved when I meet someone who is more talented than I am," Yrena went on. "I am like, 'Go! Win the competition, I will gladly come in second place!' Sometimes, I do come in second place, and my parents and teachers are disappointed. But secretly I am so happy. Unless I get competitive and I push myself harder. Then I get angry at myself for trying and succeeding."

"I'd give anything to go to one of those schools in Russia," I said. "Maybe it would give me an edge."

"You would do well there. They like passion. I can tell that you dance with passion."

"How do you know?"

"From your shoes," she said. "And I can see it in your walk. In the way that you are sitting."

The little bell over the door rang, and when I looked up, I noticed that those same two men had come inside. First one. Then the other. They were probably bored standing outside waiting for us to finish up. They ordered ice cream. They didn't sit with each other. Each sat at his own table, equally looking at each other, eyeballing us, and licking their cones. The KGB guy looked at Yrena and jutted his chin out at her as if to say *I'm watching you.*

"Creepy," I said.

"Yes," she agreed. "They will make sure that I go home soon."

"Are you afraid?" I asked.

"Not today."

I could see myself inviting her over to my house to hang out for the rest of the night. Or another night. We could order our own pizza. We could talk more.

"Well, maybe we should go home," I said.

I was a little bit wigged out by the suits because they were watching us and it was kind of intense. It made me aware of my every action. It felt weird putting the spoon in my mouth, so I finally just pushed my plate away from me.

Yrena, though, liked to take her time. It was a few more minutes until she'd finished hers and we went outside.

"I never believed that those guys hanging around our street were really KGB or CIA," I confessed. "Todd, my brother, always says that our neighborhood is so safe because of that."

"It is true," Yrena said. "That is why I've never had a real American night out. Not that I even want one. They are always watching us—where we go, who we talk to. My parents more so than me."

The two suits watched us through the glass window and

we watched them back as they got up from their respective tables. They were now hanging back a little. They sort of looked sorry about the fact that they were tailing us.

"Well, I will walk back to the house. Have fun at your party," Yrena said. "I'll wait with you for the bus."

She walked me to the bus stop, and as we were standing there, I tried to figure out a way to tell her that I wasn't going to go to the party. I was going to step back into the shadows.

"You are exactly as nice as I thought you would be," she said.

"Maybe we could hang out again sometime," I said.

Yrena got a weird look on her face that I didn't understand. She was struggling with something.

"That would be very nice if it could happen," she said.

"Sure it can," I said. "We can make it happen."

The bus pulled up right there in front of us. And as the doors opened, I turned around to tell her that I wasn't going to the party and that she should just come over to my house right then so we could watch some TV together or something.

But instead, something else happened. Yrena pushed me onto the bus with her and reached over me to put in some bus fare as the bus pulled away.

"What are you doing?" I asked.

I was totally flummoxed.

"Carpe diem?" she said.

"What?" I asked.

"Your party, is it far downtown?"

"Miss," the bus driver said to me, "you have to put your fare in."

"I've never been downtown without my parents," Yrena said. "Only once, on a school field trip to the United Nations."

"Miss, you'll have to get off at the next stop if you don't pay your fare," the bus driver said.

The light had changed and the bus was pulling away and we were going. There was no getting off now until the next stop.

"You could take me to the party," Yrena said. "That way I can see one for myself."

Once there is a crack in you, it's so easy for just a little bit of light to seep in. That's how I felt, as though little bits of light were brightening up the dark corners inside. Once light gets in, things start to grow. Feelings ripen—a tingling in my chest, a flush of excitement, a bubbling up of *happiness*.

I dug into my pocket and put the seventy-five cents into the fare box.

I was on a bus going to a party that I hadn't planned on going to with a girl I didn't really know, and I was glad.

Yrena grabbed me and we laughed and shouted and ran to the back of the bus and plopped down on the back bench seat like friends. Like *best* friends.

71

It was while I was laughing that I noticed through the back window that the suits, who had been lazily leaning against the wall of Zips ice cream store, were now running behind the bus, waving at it, trying to tell it to stop.

The two men became tiny as we moved away from them. I poked Yrena, but she just kept looking at me. She didn't even look back. Maybe it should have struck me right then to be worried. To maybe wonder if they had radios to contact other agents. But that didn't even cross my mind. Yrena seemed calm as anything.

"I've only gotten to live in Riverdale," she said matter-of-factly. "That's not the real city."

"That's crazy," I said. "You have to see New York City. It's the best city in the world."

"*One* of the best," Yrena said, teasing me.

I was about to say something like *Maybe we shouldn't go to that party*. Yrena got this look on her face. A look that said *Don't*.

"Who will be at the party?"

"People from school," I said. "Callisto and Caitlin."

"Is Callisto a boy?"

"No. She's a girl."

"But there will be boys?"

"Yes, of course," I said.

"Good," she said.

We got off at 231st Street and climbed the stairs for the subway downtown.

We were really doing this.

The train arrived in the station and the doors slid open.

I looked over my shoulder, but there were no suits following us.

From that moment on, there was no turning back.

Party on the Steps

Yrena was tracing the graffiti tags on the subway walls, her fingers making intricate loops as they followed the marks. The farther we pulled away from the Bronx, the more I think we both relaxed.

"Those are called *tags*," I said.

"Why don't they do pictures like they do on the outside of the train?" Yrena asked.

"I don't know," I said. "I think tags are just people marking their territory. Like a cat."

"This looks ugly," she said. "But on the outside, it is very exciting."

I had to agree with her. The graffiti on the outside of the trains was thrilling. People, like the mayor and my parents, called it *vandalism*, but I thought it was *art*.

Even though their calligraphy was sometimes graceful, tags seemed dirty and uninspired. I liked them better when they were used as signatures on the outside of the subways for the massive pictures, or where the letters covered the whole outside of the car, boasting. The words were written with aerosol cans so that they looked like pure, colorful art, the kind you could believe would be in a museum. You couldn't read it until you stepped back and saw the word. I could be sitting in a car with the six-foot word *BURN*, or *STAR*, or *CRASH*, with the occasional image thrown in, like a Smurf or superhero or a hot girl or Puerto Rican flag woven in with the words. Those were pieces I could get behind because they turned the monotone of the subway into something magical. I was glad that someone cared enough to go into tunnels and car yards and make something routine anything but. My first week of school I saw a car with my name on it—*ROSE* it said, with bright red flowers climbing all over the word. I took it as a sign that no matter how hard high school was, I was doing the right thing getting on that train to head downtown.

Yrena and I talked for a bit about that. She said that in Russia, the trains were clean and that they were blue. We agreed that here everything was so dirty. She said that in Moscow there was even a station that had a chandelier in it. Imagine that. I could never picture a chandelier in a New York City subway station. Most of the stations I'd been to were downright dirty and had no frills at all. Platforms with brown peed-on cement, rats you could see running around on the tracks, strange smells, and lightbulbs that flickered. There was nothing romantic about a subway station as far as I could tell. They were just in-between places, meant to be left as quickly as possible.

The wheels screeched and there was that rumble as the car shook.

"Listen," Yrena said. "It sounds like applause."

She was right. If you used your imagination, the sound of the subway moving through the tunnel sounded a little bit like an audience bursting out with joy at the end of a masterful performance.

Brava! Brava! Brava!

"Is this Manhattan?" she asked as the train came out of a tunnel and moved along a track outside for a bit.

"Yes."

"I have left the Bronx!" Yrena said.

I put my hand into the air to give her a high five. She looked at me blankly and left me hanging, so I changed my hand into a thumbs-up. She understood that and gave me a thumbs-up back.

"Here's something you would like," I said. "Near here is the Cloisters. It's a medieval castle. They brought it brick by brick from Europe. It's part of the museum where the party is, only they keep it uptown. There are unicorn tapestries and everything."

"We have a lot of medieval things in Russia," Yrena said.

"I've seen the pictures," I said, but I actually couldn't really recall any specific pictures that I'd seen of Russia. I knew that there was a place called Red Square. But I wasn't sure if it was square or red.

"I wish we could see the castle," Yrena said. "Everything outside the window is not so nice-looking."

"That's because everything is new," I said. "We are a new country. We just had our bicentennial. Maybe all of this will be beautiful in one hundred years."

"I do not think those buildings will ever be beautiful," Yrena said.

She was looking at the apartment buildings all squashed up against one another. It was dark outside and not all the streetlamps worked. You could see the light spilling out from people's windows, dotting the buildings like constellations. Sometimes, with the close buildings, you could even catch a glimpse into those strangers' lives. A living room here. A kitchen there. We watched people moving along privately in their homes as we sped by them.

"Some people say new is better," I said as we descended into the tunnels again.

"New is not better," Yrena said.

"I didn't say that *all* new was better. I never said I didn't like *old*. Besides, how does anyone know what is going to be beautiful in a thousand years?"

"No one will know," Yrena agreed.

"Exactly, and isn't Communism new? Democracy is way older than Communism, and many people on the planet think democracy is more beautiful than Communism."

Yrena turned her head away from me and looked back out the window where the view had turned to nothing.

Where was this red, white, and blue patriotism coming from? Did being with a Russian somehow make my American feelings kick in? Why had I brought up politics? Was that inevitable when two people from different places and different points of view got together? Did we have to point out all that was different about us in order to define who we were? It was very strange. I was hoping to have fun, and instead I felt defensive and irritable. I couldn't exactly form an opinion because I realized that I didn't really have one. Everything was a vague feeling I had in my head. Nebulous thoughts about bigger issues. Vagueness doesn't really help in a friendship. But now what we'd said was just out there sitting between us. I felt like if I didn't know exactly what it was that I wanted to say, maybe I should be quiet until I did know.

People came on and off the car, and while Yrena brooded, I did what I did best: people watching. Some were dressed up to go out, some were coming home from work, some were just starting work. There were old people and young people and children. There was every kind of person on an NYC subway: the woman coming home from work in her business suit but wearing comfy sneakers. The two little girls with big brown eyes in very fancy, lacy dresses with their large, round mom. The night watchman with his metal lunch box. The scary-looking guy with wet-looking hair and his agitated girlfriend. The effeminate, delicate Indian man reading Proust.

"It is very equal on the subway," Yrena said, breaking the silence. "Every kind of person."

"Yeah," I said. "A big melting pot."

"*That* is beautiful," Yrena said. "I have not seen much of very different kinds of people in my life."

We hopped off the subway at 86th Street and took the crosstown bus. Any weirdness that had cropped up for a minute between us was forgotten. Yrena liked the look of Central Park and so did I. I realized that while I'd been to Central Park plenty of times (mostly with my parents), I didn't really *know* it. I didn't really know much about downtown at all.

The Metropolitan Museum of Art was grand and gorgeous, timeless and fierce. Even Yrena stopped talking when we approached it. I could tell that she was impressed.

"It looks like your White House," she said.

"What?" I said.

"Where the president lives."

"I know what the White House is. But I don't see it." Maybe she meant the Capitol building.

"Look again," she said.

"Maybe," I said. "If you squint."

"Squint?"

I squinted my eyes for her so she could tell what I meant. She got it and squinted back at me.

"Interesting. If you squint, you can make something look like something else," she said.

"This place is filled with treasures," I said, feeling I was responsible for being some kind of tour guide. "Art treasures."

It was funny how you could suddenly have complete ownership over something. Here I was bragging about the museum, even though I hadn't actually been to the museum in a million years, and maybe only a few times at that. I realized I was starting to compile a list in my head of things to do in NYC.

Explore Central Park.

Visit the Metropolitan Museum of Art.

I had the New York pride spring in my step.

"They have some Degas dancers in there," I said. "You would like that."

There was a room with a bunch of Degas's paintings of ballet dancers. There were also statues and a lot of them were little sculptures of dancers in the various positions. I had forgotten about them until just that moment. When I was little, my mom had taken me to see them, and for a couple of years afterward I'd loved to visit them and say hello. I could remember talking to them like friends. I had names and stories about them—what their careers were like, who was in the corps de ballet, who was the prima ballerina, who died of consumption, and who had suffered from a bad love affair. The stories were only for me—I never shared them with

Daisy—and the dramatic ones were based loosely on ballets and operas I'd seen or heard of.

It was amazing what I could remember about myself when I retraced my own steps. When I thought about it, those dancers were what I thought ballet was like more than any of the pink tulle that Daisy used to try to push on me.

I told Yrena this.

"Lovely," she said.

"Yeah."

We stood and looked at the building for a minute more, and then a gaggle of kids our age started running by us toward the steps. We followed.

It may have been a world-renowned art museum during the day, but on Friday nights the steps of the Met doubled as a high school rendezvous point for hanging out and drinking. All kids were welcome. Here, private school and public school lives met on even ground.

Kids were mingling on the steps in little groups. Some sat on the edge of the fountain at the bottom of the steps. Some were gathered up on the ledge near the doors. It was a lot of standing around, like a happening waiting to happen.

"I thought it was a party," Yrena said, looking around.

"It *is* a party," I told her. I liked that it was not a regular party with a makeout corner, a bowl of chips, and music I didn't know playing on the record player.

"But this is not what I imagined."

Yrena was definitely disappointed. If she was looking for the football players and the cheerleaders, this was definitely not the right place. I couldn't even find it for her if I wanted to.

"Well, a party is a party, right?" I said.

"There is no music," she said. "No rock and roll."

"It's better to have a unique experience."

She looked at me and pouted.

I just smiled back. A smile is sometimes all it takes to be lifted. To feel brave.

"Come on," I said with a confidence that I hadn't felt in over a year. "This is where it's *at*."

I actually didn't know if this was where it was at or if it was going to be awful. But I knew I *wanted* it to be fun. And if you wanted something to be fun, there was a better chance that it actually would be.

"Do you see your friends?" Yrena asked.

I scanned the crowd. I was counting on Callisto and Caitlin showing up like they said they would.

"No," I said. "I don't see anyone yet. But it's still early."

I was more trying to convince myself than her.

"Perhaps we should introduce ourselves and meet people," Yrena said.

"Wait," I told her. I didn't know why I said wait except that I suddenly froze up. I didn't know how to just go up and talk to people. It was the difference between being on the dance floor, where you were given all the choreography, and *being* the choreographer, where you made it all up yourself. Anything could happen.

Yrena smiled at me. "If you squint, they will look just like your friends," she said.

I squinted.

I squinted so that people looked *nicer*.

"Okay," I said. "But maybe we should start by finding someone who can get us drinks?"

Yrena nodded.

I felt better with a plan. I felt more confident about asking people for something, like a drink, than just going up to strangers and inserting myself into their conversations. I had about as much experience as Yrena did at coming out to a party, but with the two of us in it together, it was a lot easier to fake.

I was just starting to feel good about the whole night, and how it might actually go okay, when I saw Daisy coming up the stairs.

Daisy.

I felt that old rush of bad heat come over me.

Of all the people that I thought might be here, Daisy wasn't one of them. Then again, this was exactly where she would be. She probably partied all the time.

I tried to duck behind Yrena and get her to walk all the way over to the other side of the steps, but Daisy caught sight of me before we could slip away. I watched in horror as she gestured to the girls she was with. They all looked in my direction and then looked away and laughed. My heart was beating fast. I wanted to run away. I think normally I would have, but I didn't want to give myself away as a weakling in front of Yrena.

I had to remind myself that Yrena didn't know me. So she didn't care about what had happened between me and Daisy.

Yrena was what I'd thought high school would be for me: a clean slate.

Out of the corner of my eye, I could see that Daisy's friends had formed a little V behind her, like she was the lead bird in a flock of geese going south for the winter.

I stayed put and tried to size up who would be the best person to approach for booze.

"Are those your friends coming toward us?" Yrena asked. She'd noticed Daisy's crowd looking at us.

"I wouldn't call them friends," I said.

"But you know them?"

"I used to go to school with them." That sounded like a nice balance between a lie and the truth. "They go to Science."

She didn't know what that meant. So I explained.

"They go to a school called Bronx Science. My brother goes there, too."

"Maybe they will have a drink for us," she said, starting toward them.

"No," I said a little too forcefully, and tried to catch her arm. But I missed and watched as she moved down the steps toward Daisy and her friends. I forced myself to follow, pretending I was making an entrance from the wings onto a stage. *Listen to the music. And one, two, three, go.*

When Yrena and I reached Daisy's spot on the steps, she hemmed us in like she was afraid we'd get away. It seemed strategic, and I remembered that she was always doing stuff like that, forcing me into the weaker position.

"Hello," Yrena said, extending her hand into a handshake. "I am Yrena. Rose's friend."

"Rose," Daisy said as she eyeballed Yrena and ignored her extended hand. "It's so *weird* to see you here. I never see you out at anything fun."

"I run in different circles now," I said.

"Must be a small circle," she shot back.

"Yrena, this is Daisy," I said. "We used to go to school together."

"You mean we used to be friends," Daisy said.

"I am Yrena," Yrena said again.

"Yrena," Daisy said. "Great name. So you go to Performing Arts?"

"Go?" Yrena said blankly.

"Where do you go?" Daisy was losing patience — and she didn't have much to start with. "What *high school* do you go to? Are you at Performing Arts, too?"

"She doesn't go anywhere," I said. "We live next door to each other."

"I thought those weird commies lived next door," Daisy said.

I cringed. It had sounded funny when we referred to the next-door neighbors as "commies" when Daisy and I were in eighth grade, but out loud, now, it made me feel embarrassed.

"I didn't know you guys had become friends," Daisy went on. "I guess desperate times . . ."

No matter how much I kept the smile on my face and no matter how much I tried to just pretend that I didn't feel anything, I still felt wounded.

How is it, I wondered, *that you can be best friends with someone for such a long time and then, when you break it off, you still know so much about them, and so little at the same time? And how, despite all that distance, can she still get to me in a way that no one else can?*

Yrena was standing next to me with her arms crossed, totally at ease. Any intimidation that Daisy and her posse were trying to force on me completely passed over Yrena's head.

I realized I had something I'd never had when confronted by Daisy before.

I had backup.

Since I felt like I was performing, I moved forward with a new plan. The plan was that I was fabulous and that I had a friend in Yrena and that I was excited about being out, which was true, and that I wasn't going to let Daisy bother me.

All of that gave me a tiny push to be a little bit different than I normally was. Daisy was staring at me. It was my line, my solo, my turn.

"We're looking for a bottle," I said.

"It's BYOB," Daisy said. "Tough luck."

"There's twenty bucks in it for you if you can find some," I said. "I bet you could get some for us."

"I thought you didn't drink," Daisy said. "I thought you were, like, a Goody Two-ballet-shoes."

"We don't care what it is," I pushed on. I'd never said that I didn't drink.

"I think now maybe you can go help us get something to drink, yes?" Yrena said.

"I can get you some beer, or maybe a little bottle of hard alcohol," Daisy said, giving in not to me, but to Yrena.

"We don't care what it is," I said.

I slid Daisy the twenty and she went up the steps a bit, over to a guy who looked like he was a senior.

I watched as she flirted with the senior-looking guy till he opened up his trench coat and handed her something. She gave him a big hug and then came back over to us, brandishing two bottles like trophies in her hands.

"Rum and Coke," she said.

I didn't really want to keep hanging out with Daisy and her Science friends, so I thanked her politely and led Yrena a few steps away. I opened the rum, then pretended to take a sip and chase it down with a big gulp of Coke. After I was through, I passed the bottles over to Yrena, who made a face at the taste of the rum.

I thought we'd go back and forth like this. But instead Yrena walked over and passed the rum to Daisy next.

"Uh, no," Daisy said.

"We must share," Yrena insisted. "It is the friendly thing to do."

Daisy shocked me again by reaching out for the rum and taking a swig. The bottle of Coke exploded a bit on her shirt when she opened it.

Yrena smiled, but didn't laugh.

"Good," she said. "Now we are all friends."

I didn't want to say that Daisy and I would never be friends again. And neither did Daisy. We let our disagreement hang between us like a wall. It had nothing to do with Yrena.

"Oh my God, here he comes," Daisy suddenly turned and squealed to one of her friends.

I looked over my shoulder, curious to see who she was looking at. It was a hippie-looking guy in a Guatemalan shirt. He was approaching us with a kind of I'm-on-a-tropical-island gait. He had longish, wavy blond hair and a beard. He was wearing an old-style hat that made him look cool, even though it shouldn't have.

"Hey there," he said.

Daisy moved over a little bit so that now she was kind of standing with us again. All the Science girls flipped their hair a little.

"Hi, Free," Daisy said.

But Free was looking straight at Yrena.

"Hello — I don't know you, do I?" he said.

"Free, this is Rose and Yrena," Daisy said. She had that look in her eyes like she totally wanted to get with that guy and she was glad that he was standing near her because of us, but mad that he'd noticed us and not her.

"Free?" Yrena said.

"Is that your name or your nickname?" I asked.

"My name," Free said in a tired way, like he got that all the time.

Yrena started to laugh and then tried to swallow it like she knew it wasn't right to laugh at someone's name.

"My parents were hippies," Free explained.

"But to name a child *Free*?" Yrena said.

"It's just my name," he said. "Everyone has to be called something."

"There's a girl in my class named Winter. And one named Echo," Daisy said, trying to insert herself back into the conversation.

"That is also very funny," Yrena said. Still, she wasn't laughing. She had a serious look on her face.

"Truth is, when I was a kid I wanted to be called Bob," Free said.

"Bob!" Now Yrena *was* almost laughing. She allowed herself once Free started laughing, too.

"I know, ridiculous!" he said.

His eyes were on Yrena and me, and I could tell that Daisy was about to have a conniption fit. Maybe it made me kind of mean, but I enjoyed seeing Daisy denied what she wanted. It was nice to see her have to work a little. I watched with pleasure as Daisy had to move down a few steps and then move around so that he could see her again.

"Who are you?" Free asked.

"Yrena."

Free could tell that there was something different about Yrena because he leaned in close to her and then took her hands, like she was a princess or something. She looked more like a czarina than a worker.

She allowed her hands to be taken.

"Where are you from? I love your accent," he said, like he'd discovered gold. He wasn't at all mad that she had made fun of his name. He was *intrigued.*

From where I was standing, I could see that Free's eyes were the kind of brown that made him look like he was sensitive and cared about the whole world. At the very least, he cared about whales.

"I am from Russia."

"'Without a revolutionary theory there cannot be a revolutionary movement,'" Free said.

"Lenin," Yrena said.

"I read," Free said.

Free reached into his bag and took out a flyer. "Hey,

there's a No Nukes rally tomorrow in Central Park," he said. "You should meet me there."

"I'll meet you there," Daisy said.

"Great," Free said, ignoring Daisy and putting the flyer into Yrena's hands. "See you all there."

Then he moved on to another group of people to hand out more flyers.

"I don't need a flyer 'cause I'll probably just go with him tomorrow," Daisy said. "Free is on the Ultimate Frisbee team. I go to all the games."

I wanted to get away from Daisy. I looked around to see if Callisto and Caitlin had arrived, and that's when I saw Maurice Tibbets running up the stairs. He wasn't coming toward me, he was going toward another group of drama girls. I knew they were drama girls not only because one of them was Tammy, the girl from the pizza parlor, and not only because I saw Stanley trying unsuccessfully to insert himself into their circle, but because they were acting theatrical in their drunkenness, and drunk in their theatricality.

Maurice, however, looked graceful when he ran. Powerful. No wonder he could dance circles around anyone if he could take the steps two at a time that effortlessly. He was probably a better dancer than Martins, Baryshnikov, Nureyev, and d'Amboise all rolled into one.

Struck by the moment, I did the unimaginable. I called out to him.

"Maurice!" I yelled. "We're over here!"

I tugged on Yrena's arm and it looked like she could tell it was because I wanted to get away from Daisy and the Science girls. I could tell by the look on her face that she was ready to go, too. On that front, we were united.

Maurice stopped running toward the drama girls when he heard his name. He looked around while he tried to figure out who was calling to him, and then his eyes fell on me. He seemed a bit stunned and confused, since I had never hung out with him or his group. I had never spoken more than two sentences in a row to him, and most of those sentences were "Was that a grand jeté?" "On two or three?" "Right foot first?"

Yrena waved. I followed her lead and waved really big, like we said hello to him all the time. Daisy looked intrigued by what I was doing.

Maurice stuck his hand up uncertainly and waved back to us before continuing on to the drama girls. When he got to them and said his hellos, I noticed that he turned back and looked at me again with curiosity. The drama girls all craned their necks to get a look at me, and I smiled back at them all and waved again, like I was cool. Because I was smiling, they started smiling, and Maurice waved me over just like we really were friends.

"Let's go," I said.

"Who's that?" Daisy asked, not even bothering to hide her interest.

"Is that your boy friend?" Yrena asked.

I knew from the way that Yrena said it she meant a friend who was a boy, but Daisy didn't know that.

"Boyfriend?" Daisy said. "You have a boyfriend, Rose? I wasn't aware that hell had frozen over."

"He's just over there," Yrena said, pointing over at Maurice. I didn't want to answer any of the questions that were forming on Daisy's lips.

"Bye, Daisy," I said.

Yrena took the bottles out of Daisy's hands and we walked away.

"Your friends are strange," Yrena said. "I do not like them very much."

"I don't go to school with them. They're not really my friends now."

I got nervous again. We were leaving one person who wasn't my friend but who I actually knew, and approaching another one who wasn't my actual friend but I probably liked more. Each step that we took was a step closer to me being one hundred percent humiliated. Maurice wasn't even close to being an acquaintance. I wasn't even sure he'd remember my name.

"I'm not exactly friends with Maurice," I warned Yrena. "I just wanted to get away from Daisy."

"Oh," Yrena said, smiling impishly.

"Maurice is a dancer. He's in my class."

"I understand. No problem."

I didn't know exactly what it was that she understood, but I was sure that she wasn't going to embarrass me, and that was all I really cared about. Despite being from the total other side of the planet, Yrena seemed to have all the social skills that I lacked.

"Are those people with him your friends?" Yrena asked.

"They're from my school," I said, which was not a lie. "But Callisto and Caitlin—the friends I was meeting—aren't here yet."

"I am so curious about your arts school," Yrena said.

We got right up to the drama girls and stood there for a second, not really saying anything. Then Yrena did the craziest thing—she gave each one of them a big hug and a kiss like they were her best friends. She kissed them all on the cheek three times, like she was French or something, and even though I had never talked to Maurice, I nodded to him like it was no big deal and I did it all the time. I just pretended.

"Rose." Maurice said it slowly, like he was unsure, but sure.

"We're in dance together," I said, trying to find something to talk about.

"I know," he replied. "How about that combination in Mr. Heath's class?"

"That was something else. Modern isn't my thing," I said. "I couldn't get my contraction to snap."

"You have to do it from the center, like this," he said, and

94

then he did a perfect contraction. He snapped his body like every single muscle in it was a separate thing that he had complete control over.

"Show it again," Yrena said.

Maurice repeated the move. Yrena looked at him very carefully and then she repeated the movement perfectly.

"Nice," he said. He held up his hand to do a high five . . . and Yrena gave him a thumbs-up.

"She's Russian," I said, as though that explained everything.

He went from looking like he felt a bit dumb for being left hanging to relieved, because it wasn't like he was being dissed or anything.

"Russian, huh?" He took Yrena's hand and showed her how to slap it in a high five. She liked it. So then she high-fived me and Tammy, too.

I was feeling good—until Tammy asked, "Is your sweater on backward?" I felt myself turning bright red, but then Tammy added, "I'm totally going to bite that off of you. You don't mind, do you?"

I looked down and remembered that I wasn't wearing anything that I usually wore. I looked a bit funkier than usual.

"Go crazy," I said.

"Cool," Tammy said.

The other drama kids crowded around me and clucked in approval. Somehow, after two months of being on the outside, they were treating me as though I was in.

"You'll totally have to teach me how to dress like you do," Tammy said. "I'm really into being kind of New Wave. Cigarette?"

She passed me a Dunhill Blue.

"No, thanks—I don't smoke," I said.

"I thought all the dancers smoked!" Tammy said.

"I don't smoke," Maurice said.

"Well, not you, Maurice!" Tammy said, playfully squeezing his arm.

Maurice had strong arms. Nice veins. He must have had those arms from all the partnering he did. I could just imagine what those arms would be like lifting me. I couldn't stop looking at them. In truth, he wasn't my type. I would've bet that most people wouldn't have understood that. I didn't want to get with him. I just would have killed to be partnered with him in a dance.

"I will take a cigarette," Yrena said. "But I don't want this one. I want an American one. A Marlboro."

Someone passed over a Camel Light to Yrena, who put it in her mouth and lit it up.

In all the time I'd watched her in her room, I'd never seen her sneak a cigarette. Now she looked like she knew what she was doing—she didn't cough or anything. But still, to me, the cigarette didn't look natural in her hands or mouth.

"I smoke because it's an appetite suppressant," Tammy volunteered. "I'm so skinny because whenever I'm hungry, I just smoke! And you know, actresses need to be thin, right, Maurice?"

"How would I know?" he said.

"Because of your mom?" Tammy said. "She does all those diet commercials."

Maurice looked away.

Tammy didn't pick up on it. "Isn't this party great? We come every Friday." She'd squeezed her way in between me and Yrena. She stood very close to Maurice. He took a step back away from her.

"I've never seen you here before, Rose," he said.

"Doesn't mean a girl can't show up," I said.

Free came bursting in.

"Hey again," he said. "Just wanted to make sure that your friends knew about the No Nukes rally."

He handed Maurice a flyer, which I hadn't even looked at closely. It said: REVERSE THE ARMS RACE. NO NUKES RALLY — OCTOBER 30TH, 1982, CENTRAL PARK 11 A.M. TILL SUNSET.

"That's tomorrow," Maurice said. Then he turned to me. "You gonna go?"

"I've been thinking about it," I said, even though I hadn't been thinking about it at all.

"Maybe I could meet you there," Maurice said. "No Nukes is important."

"A protest?" Tammy interjected. "That sounds really hard."

"Well," Maurice said, "it sounds like it's important."

"Caleb Mazzeretti and all the stoners are doing some kind of skit there," Stanley said, trying to insert himself into the conversation by acting like he was in the know. "They've been practicing all week."

"Boring," Tammy said.

"That's cool. Caleb Mazzeretti is pretty cool," Maurice said. "You're friends with him, right, Rose?"

"No," I said. "But I know his sisters. I was supposed to meet them here."

"Hey, Yrena," Free said. "Do you want to walk around the side of the building? You can see the Egyptian temple all lit up."

Free took Yrena's hand and I looked at Maurice. He nodded and we followed them as they quickly moved down the stairs and away from the drama girls.

I looked back over my shoulder, expecting Tammy to be seething. But instead she just turned to two of the other girls, laughing and talking in a perfect, tight little group. I was a little jealous that they had that. They were huddled together in a way that made them look like one body with three heads, like something that would be in *The Odyssey*. Or maybe more like those three witches from *Macbeth*.

We hit the sidewalk that curved around the building. There, behind the path, were enormous windows, and through them we could see the Egyptian temple. Yrena and Free moved ahead of us and pushed through the bushes to get up close to the glass, which was really dirty and covered with people's names written in the dust. Maurice and I joined them and we all stood there, hands pressed against the glass, breathing together, leaving perfect handprints. The temple looked as though it were in a cage. I wanted to smash the glass and set it free, but why bother? Transported stones cannot go home. They rest where they have been dragged to. That building would sit at the edge of Central Park for eternity.

"Do you actually go to museums? Or do you just drink on the steps and never go inside?" Yrena asked.

"I used to come here more," I said. "There's a good book about two kids who run away and live in there."

"Oh, I read that book in fifth grade," Maurice said. "I love that book."

"I liked that they were here at night," I said. "Sleeping on the old beds. Wandering through the art."

"We are here at night," Yrena said. "We are like your book."

"I've partied more on its steps at night than gone inside during the day," Free admitted.

"Tell me what is in there," Yrena asked.

"Everything," Maurice said.

"Endless rooms of Greek statues and Chinese vases," Free said.

"And paintings, so many paintings," I said. "Beautiful furniture, photographs."

"It would take days to see everything," Free said.

"Weeks," I said.

"Years." Maurice smiled.

Yrena snorted.

"What?" I asked.

"You have the freedom to come here whenever you want and instead of coming to enjoy the actual treasures, you treasure your time outside talking," she said.

"You were the one looking for a party," I pointed out.

"A regular party, with disco music," she said.

"We're at a party on the steps of the Metropolitan Museum of Art. We are artistic just by being here. We are the works of art," I said.

"I like that," Maurice said. "I really like that! I don't need to be inside because I am a work of art!"

But Yrena and Free didn't care anymore, because while Maurice was turned to me, they had started kissing.

"Uh-oh," Maurice said. "I think they want to be alone."

"I can't leave her alone," I said.

"Come on, I'll walk you to the tunnel to give them a few minutes and then come back for them. Also — it embarrasses me to say this — but I really, really have to pee."

"Me, too, actually," I said.

I headed off with Maurice into the park. As we turned the bend, I looked over my shoulder and saw that Yrena and Free had stopped kissing and were writing in the dust on the museum window.

"You go first," Maurice said when we got to one of the tunnels in the park. "I'll stand here."

The tunnel was creepy and dark. It smelled like pee already. I'd never thought of myself as the kind of girl who would go to a party and pee in a tunnel, but there I was, squatting and trying not to get pee on my shoes. I laughed.

"You okay? Or is that a signal?" Maurice asked.

"No, I'm laughing," I said. I pulled up my underwear and then emerged from the mouth of the tunnel. I felt lighter and better.

"Stand watch for me," Maurice said.

Once he was done, we walked back to get Yrena and Free and rejoin the party. Maurice and I started talking dance — specifically, about remedies for blisters on your feet. Even Free had some ideas about foot care. His advice for athlete's foot? Use a mixture of honey and garlic slathered over the foot. Sounded pretty gummy and potentially yummy. We all agreed we'd try it.

When we breezed by Daisy and the Science girls, I didn't get that knot in my stomach again. I didn't cringe as she threw dagger-eyes at me. Or at least I didn't cringe *much*.

"I have an idea," Yrena said, grabbing my arm and dashing me down the steps, away from the boys so she could talk to me alone. She stuck her hand into her pocket and pulled out the flyer.

"That's tomorrow," I said.

"I know," she said. "We will stay out all night!"

I shook my head. "I can maybe stay at this party for a little while longer, but I definitely can't stay out all night."

"But I do not want to go home yet. Now I want to see the sun rise. Now I want to go to the march."

"Yrena," I said, "we can go together tomorrow if you want. We just need to go home to sleep."

"There is no other way," Yrena said.

"ROSE!" two voices cried.

There, coming up the steps with swagger, were Callisto and Caitlin. Still calling my name, they ran over. Callisto looked David Bowie–perfect and Caitlin looked dramatic in a black pencil skirt and cute fifties sweater.

When they reached me, they both gave me a big hug.

"I can't believe you made it," Caitlin said.

"I think I have to go soon," I said.

"You can't go," Callisto said. "We just got here!"

Yrena was mad. I could hear her as she stomped away from me, back up the stairs to Free. I turned back to Callisto and Caitlin.

"Who's that sourpuss?" Caitlin asked.

"She looks like she's sucking on lemons," Callisto said.

"That's Yrena," I said. "She's my next-door neighbor. She's never been downtown before. Not without some supervision."

"Never?" Callisto said. "That's weird. I mean, that's really weird."

"She's from the Soviet Union," I said. "For real, not like a defector. She lives next door to me and her parents do something at the consulate. Maybe they're spies. I don't know."

"You don't know?" Caitlin asked.

"No," I said. "She's lived next door to me for two years and I've never spoken to her before tonight."

"So, let me get this straight," Callisto said. "My sister and I ask you to go out and you say no. But some girl from the USSR who you don't even know asks you and you say yes?"

I started getting a little queasy. I felt as though I had done something bad and no matter what I said it was going to come out sounding wrong.

"I meant to say yes to you," I said.

Callisto threw her arms up in the air aggressively.

"I feel like I'm mad at you," she said.

"Oh, no. No. No. Please don't be mad at me," I said.

"Ugh," Callisto said, and surprised me by pulling me in for a hug. "I'm not really mad."

"But I'm just a little hurt," Caitlin said.

"I'm sorry," I said. "I meant to say yes. I just couldn't."

"I know! You're like the Rock of Gibraltar! Keeping all your good stuff to yourself," Caitlin said.

"Forget it," Callisto told me. "Let's get this party started. Let me have a sip of that bottle of something."

I passed her the rum and the Coke. She took a swig of each and let out a little whoop. Then she passed the bottles over to Caitlin and put her arms around my shoulders and pulled me up the steps.

"Let's see who's here," she said.

We got a good vantage point so we could suss out the party.

"Nerds at twelve o'clock." Caitlin pointed to a bunch of awkward boys standing together with their hands in their pockets. They looked like my brother and his friends.

"Stuyvesant, UNIS, Fieldston, Hunter, Science," Callisto said, pointing at a different group on each step.

"Punks, New Wavers, jocks, brains, sluts," Caitlin said, pointing to other groups on other steps.

"Good, then—looks like everyone is here," Callisto concluded, jostling me in a friendly way.

"Let's go join the PA'ers," Caitlin said.

I started scanning the steps for Yrena, who I'd last seen standing with Free.

"I don't see her," I said.

"Who?" Caitlin asked.

"Yrena, the girl I'm here with."

"She was over there earlier," Callisto said.

"I know, but now I don't see her. I don't see Free, either."

"Well, maybe they went to go make out," Caitlin said. "It's hard to do that on the steps."

"You're right. Or maybe they're at the tunnel, to pee," I said.

We walked to the back and saw plenty of people on the side of the building making out or smoking pot, but not Yrena. The only thing that was left of her was her name written in the dust on the window.

"Don't worry about it," Caitlin said. "We'll find her."

I wasn't so convinced. She'd vanished into thin air.

Back at the steps, I made a beeline for Maurice.

"We're looking for Yrena," I said. "Have you seen her?"

"She said good-bye," Maurice told me.

I started to freak out.

"Hey, Rose." Daisy was standing there. She had her hand on her hip and she was looking angry. "Your friend is a bitch."

"What?"

"I made out with Free last week at Jen's party," Daisy said. "I had dibs. And then I see her getting into a cab, leaving with Free and a couple of your PA friends."

"Oh, that's right—I think they went with Tammy to the rock," Maurice said.

"The rock?" I said. "How could she leave me like that?"

"Yrena wanted to go to another party," Maurice said. "And Tammy wanted to hang out with the drama people."

"Come on, Rose," Daisy said. "You should just bail on that girl and this party and come home with me. We could share a cab."

"I have to think," I said, a little startled by the offer.

"I'm trying to help you," Daisy said, put off. "You should be nice."

I almost said I was sorry. I almost believed that Daisy really wanted to make up with me. But then I realized she probably just wanted to pump me for information about Yrena. And for the first time since we had stopped being friends, I didn't miss her. I didn't care for her.

"I have to go to the rock," I said. "I have to go find her."

"I know where it is," Callisto said.

I turned away from Daisy. I could imagine her cursing me out as soon as I was out of earshot.

"Come on. We'll help you go get her," Maurice said.

"You mean you guys will come with me?" I said.

"Of course," Caitlin said.

"What did you think?" Callisto said.

I'd thought I was all alone.

The Rock

Maurice was already standing in the street with his arm in the air, waving down a yellow cab.

"Can't we walk?" I said.

"Through Central Park?" Callisto said.

"At night?" Caitlin asked.

"Don't worry. I have money," Maurice said, and we piled into the taxi.

I was squashed in the middle, trying to keep it together.

I'd thought Yrena was my friend. And now instead of having fun, she had put me in a bad situation—without even saying good-bye. I was going to be in a lot of trouble if I didn't find her.

I had never been in trouble before, not really. I was a pretty good girl—not the Goody Two-ballet-shoes in Daisy's mind, but not the kind of girl who got into the trouble I was imagining that I was going to be facing if I didn't find Yrena and bring her back home.

I tried to calculate just how much trouble I could possibly get in. Probably a lot of trouble. So much trouble that I would be grounded forever. So much trouble that I wouldn't get to go to college. So much trouble that I would likely have to live at home for the rest of my life and never be allowed to go on a date and end up as an old maid.

After all, I'd lost a whole human being.

I glanced out the window as we weaved in and out of traffic. The streetlights illuminated parts inside the cab. My hands. Callisto's face. Maurice's hair. Caitlin's earrings.

"Can you go faster?" I asked the cab driver.

Even though I'd lived in New York City my whole life, I didn't know where I was. Somewhere on the East Side, going downtown, was all I knew. If you'd asked me to point to it on a map, I would have failed.

I adjusted myself, trying to settle in. But I couldn't relax. The pressure of trying to be cool in front of Maurice, Caitlin, and Callisto, who were acting like they actually liked me, was killing me.

"Why does your face look like that?" Maurice asked. I was squashed up next to him and he massaged my shoulders, like we did to one another in the warm-up exercise in the one acting class we had to take. Usually it felt nice, but now I was freaking out. "That's how you look in dance class."

"Like what?" I asked. But as I spoke, I realized that I had been holding my face in a grimace. No matter how I spun it, I knew it didn't look very pretty.

I knew that I was not very pretty.

"All angry or something," Maurice said. "Your face gets all frozen."

I didn't know if I liked the fact that he'd noticed my face in class. Or that I even did the face in class. It struck me that I felt that same mix of angry at myself and totally terrified whenever I was overwhelmed and out of my comfort zone.

There was no space outside. On one side of the street, buildings were pressed up next to one another, block after block. Only the green of the park on the other side gave some relief. Cars were honking. The taxi made a sharp turn. I fell into Maurice. He pushed me back up.

In class, everything went so fast and everyone was so on top of everything that it took every ounce of concentration to keep it together and keep up. Just like that moment right then in the cab. The night was slipping out of my fingers.

"Here, here," Callisto said, banging on the plastic divide. The cab driver pulled over and we emerged from the cab at the bottom edge of Central Park.

"I gotta make a phone call," I said, spotting a bay of pay phones. I left them standing there paying for the cab.

I had never been so happy that my parents gave Todd his own telephone for his own room. That's what I wanted for my sixteenth birthday. But I wanted mine to be a rotary phone. Black. Todd had an orange one with push buttons. He thought it looked futuristic.

I slid the dime into the slot and dialed the number.

Come on. Come on. Come on.

Pick up. Pick up. Pick up.

"You've reached Todd. Rhymes with *Zod*. Land of Nod. And alien pod. Leave your transmission at the tone. May the Force be with you."

"Todd. Are you there? Pick up."

The phone clicked as someone picked up.

"This is Dungeon Master Hertreopo," Todd said in a booming voice. "What do you want, Rose? And don't say we're making too much noise down here because I know you can't hear us from upstairs. The garage is *soundproof.*"

"I'm not calling from upstairs," I said.

Todd was quiet for a moment.

"Really? You went out?" He sounded impressed. "Where are you calling from?"

"Central Park South and Sixth Avenue."

"Whoa!"

I could hear his lame-o friends in the background yelling at him to get back to the game.

"I need your help," I said.

"You need my help," he said. "Oh, how I like the sound of this. *Hey! Don't touch that troll! And don't move your dwarf into that hexagon until your turn!*"

I imagined he and his friends were wearing costumes. God. I was going to owe Todd one forever. His nasal breathing on the phone reminded me that he was the last person I wanted to owe one to. I was beginning to regret calling now.

"Have you noticed if the girl next door came home?" I asked.

"You mean Yrena, my love?"

"Yes, Yrena."

"No, I haven't noticed her. Besides, I've been playing D&D, and I don't think that she goes out much. What's going on?"

"I took her to a party."

"You *what?*"

"I took her to a party."

"And you didn't invite me along?"

"You were busy with your dungeons. And your dragons."

"You are hanging out with *Yrena!* Screw the dragons!"

I could believe that Yrena would be the only thing that would distract Todd from his fantasy world, because she was his ultimate fantasy.

"Wait. Are you lying?" he asked.

I was about to lose my patience. "I'm not lying."

"Wow. Did she ask about me?"

"A little," I said.

"Really?" Todd said excitedly. "I wasn't expecting that to be your answer! What did she say?"

"Not much," I said.

"Okay, but you made me sound cool, right? I need details."

"Todd, I'm in a rush."

"You said you needed my help. The price for help is details."

I scrolled over the things that Yrena had said about Todd to try to come up with something that would satisfy him and not let him know that there had been a moment in a parallel universe when she could have been the only girl at his D&D party.

"She said that you seemed like you had fun," I said.

"Nice," he said. "Tell her I think the color blue looks good on her."

"I can't."

"Why not? Just tell her that fuzzy blue sweater she wore last week when she was in her garden looked great. Ask her if she bought it at a store or if she knit it herself."

"I can't," I repeated. "She's not here."

"So she's not with you right now? Right this second? Call her over. I want to say hello."

"No, I can't do that," I said, closing my eyes because it felt easier to tell the truth that way. "Because I've lost her."

"Hang on."

Cue: mumbling and rustling.

"Tyler says that there is a lot of activity next door. You know. With those suits."

"KGB or CIA?"

"I don't know, I can't see their eyebrows."

In a moment of panic, that made me smile.

"Rose. Those diplomatic kids are pretty isolated and insulated. She probably doesn't even know how to get back home. You've got to find her."

"Fine. Just keep a lookout and I'll call you back in a bit."

"Yeah, okay," Todd said.

"Don't say anything to Mom and Dad," I added.

"They'd have to torture me first. And I have studied techniques . . ."

"Okay, bye." I hung up the phone. I didn't want to hear about Todd's techniques for withstanding torture.

I started sweating.

I had to find someone, like a needle in a haystack. I was looking into the park, and I realized that as much as it sucked, New York City was a pretty amazing haystack.

Walking into the park at night was a bit magical. Like going into the forest that surrounds Sleeping Beauty's castle. That was a part that I would like to dance, the Lilac Fairy. I suppose most people would want to be Princess Aurora, but I think ever since I saw the breathtaking performance of it at the American Ballet Theater with Natalia Makarova and Mikhail Baryshnikov, it was Martine van Hamel as the Lilac Fairy and Fernando Bujones as the Bluebird who thrilled me the most. I thought, in the end, that the Lilac Fairy had the biggest heart in the story and that was the kind of fairy that I wanted to be. I never minded afterward when Daisy and I played at being prima ballerina and she would insist on being the princesses and make me be all the other parts. Often it was the other parts that got the more interesting movements of music.

It was quiet once we entered the park, the sounds of the city fading a bit to the background. As we stepped deeper into the park, we began to hear the party before we saw it.

Laughter.

Bottles rolling on the ground.

Squeals.

A rap.

"My name is Zizi or Zizzle D and I'm here with my friend Emily. We've got a little rap to do for you. About the girl who's a popular screw . . ."

And then I saw it. It was really just a big old rock with kids standing everywhere on it. On the ground there were brown bags filled with snacks and six-packs of beer. Only this was just kids from Performing Arts, not from every school in the city. It was more gritty than the museum party. More mixed. Less elite feeling.

Mostly it was older kids. Juniors and seniors. And then the cooler freshmen and sophomores. All kids from all the departments were hanging out together.

When we got to the bottom of the rock, some kids turned to check us out, then turned back to what they were doing. Some of them waved. They knew we belonged.

Caitlin grabbed me.

"Look, it's David Freddy and Elliot Waldman. Let's start with them."

They were sitting, legs stretched out, passing a joint between them with a bunch of kids sitting around them looking worshipful.

One of them was Caleb.

"Hi," Caitlin said a little breathlessly. "We're looking for our friend, a Russian girl . . ."

"If you want to be in the skit, sit down," Elliot said. "We'll see if we can fit you in."

Caitlin immediately sat down.

"No way," Caleb protested. "They can't be in the skit."

"We don't want to be in the skit," Callisto said.

"Well, I don't know," Caitlin said.

"This is *my* place," Caleb said.

"It's a rock in Central Park," Callisto said. "You don't own it."

"We're looking for my friend," I said. "A Russian girl."

"Who are you again?" Caleb asked. His brown hair was longer than short and shorter than long and parted just off center in a cowlick that made what could be considered average looks unaverage. He was skinny and wore a brown T-shirt with an army jacket and a pair of faded blue jeans. His eyes were dark hazel and serious. His lips were full and he had scruff on his cheeks, and in my opinion he looked like he was always scowling. It was probably just a side effect of his deep thoughts and drama department broodiness.

"Rose," I said.

"Oh yeah—the one who throws things at me," he said.

"The Russian girl would have come with that girl Tammy and some Science kids," Maurice said.

"Tammy. Is she one of the goblin girls with the antique dresses and green hair? Smoking cloves?" Elliot asked.

We all nodded.

Elliot jerked his thumb over his shoulder to another part of the rock.

"Get her and leave please. This is my scene," Caleb said.

Then he grabbed a beer from a brown shopping bag on the ground and cracked it open.

As we started to walk away, Caleb called after us.

"Rose. I can see your underwear."

"Your brother is a jerk," I said.

"I know," Callisto told me.

"Imagine having to share a womb with him," Caitlin added.

We made our way over to a bunch of girls all looking vintage-y perfect in their antique dresses and kid gloves. I didn't see Yrena, but Tammy was sitting with them on the ground, trying to fit in.

"Hey! Maurice! I knew you would change your mind and join us," she said, standing up as soon as she saw us. She wobbled a bit, totally tanked, and then stumbled over.

"Maurice," she said. She pulled him into a big hug and clung on to him for a little bit too long. "I'm so glad you came. I like you so much."

Maurice peeled her off of his shoulders.

"We're looking for Yrena," he said. "Have you seen her?"

"Oh, she went home," Tammy said.

"Are you sure?" I asked.

"I think so. I don't know! I don't even know her," Tammy said. "I wish I could just go home. Just right now. Like Dorothy."

Then Tammy clicked her heels three times but lost her balance and fell flat on her butt. She threw her arms up in the air dramatically.

"Help me up, Maurice!" she said. As he did so, she added, "I remember now. They went to the owl place." Even when she was up, she still tried to hold Maurice's hand.

"What's the owl place?" I asked.

"Maurice, where does your mom keep her Oscar? Can I come over to your house and touch it?"

"Sure," Maurice said. "If you tell me where the owl place is."

One of the green goblin girls started laughing and talking to us.

"Night Birds," she yelled at us.

"Where?" I asked.

"Night Birds," Maurice said. "It's a drama hangout."

"Oh yeah, Night Birds," Tammy mumbled to herself.

"Second Avenue between Fifth and Sixth," Callisto said. "I know where that is."

"Was she with Free?" I asked Tammy.

"What do you mean, is it free? It's a *bar*," she said, and laughed, like she thought I was dumb or something. Then she turned to Maurice in an about-face and acted all sweet and syrupy. "Can I come with you guys?"

"Maybe another time," he said. "The cab is full now."

"Oh," Tammy said. Then she put her hand up to her mouth and ran off to throw up.

"Come on — we know where she went," Callisto said.

"Shh," Caitlin said.

The kids in Caleb's group were standing up and doing their skit when we approached. Caitlin had drifted over before us and was watching the actors and encouraging them.

Two drama kids were wearing top hats and fake drawn-on mustaches. They froze into a position, like they were mannequins. There was rustling in the "backstage" area, which was really just another rock. Some girls wearing crinolines over their jeans were jostling one another and trying to remember what they were supposed to do.

Elliot Waldman gave them a cue and the girls pushed Caleb forward. He stepped between the two kids in top hats, who nodded that he was in the right place. The girls giggled. Caleb shot them a *shut up* look and cleared his throat.

"Step right up, step right up, and see for yourself, the two largest bullies in the world beat the living crap out of each other. You can have a front row ticket to the end of the world!"

Caleb's whole broody personality changed once his mouth opened. Now he was acting like an emcee with an old-timey voice.

"Hello, I'm the USSR and I hate you," one kid said.

"Hello, I'm the USA and I hate you," another kid said.

Then they put up their fists and pretended to box as though they were in the 1920s.

"These boys are going to put on a real show for you. Fireworks, fisticuffs, and everything. It's going to be the big bang," Caleb said. "Who will win? No one knows. I'm taking all bets. The cost to play? Your GNP. Cheap. Cheap. Cheap. Make your bets!"

"'I'm going to get you!'" one boy prompted. "'With my bombs!'"

The USSR repeated the line.

Then each of them, the USSR and the USA, slapped their hands, and the girls came out and did some sort of weird dance move, shaking their colorful crinolines and doing what sort of looked like a cancan to make it seem like their skirts were explosions while they made bomb noises.

The actors stopped what they were doing.

"It's lame," Caleb said.

"It'll be fine!" Elliot Waldman said. "It's good. Keep going."

"Come on, let's go," I said.

The actors continued dancing and making bomb explosions behind us as we left the rock.

"Are the girls supposed to be the bombs?" Callisto asked.

"Yeah, it's very avant-garde," Caitlin said. "They're going to perform it at that rally tomorrow."

I wasn't sure they were going to change very many minds, but I kept my opinion to myself. I was in my own avant-garde international incident performance. The one where the girl next door was lost downtown. Where, in my mind, there could be KGB swarming all over Yrena's house already, like roaches in the bathroom. I didn't know how the piece ended. Or what would happen if she didn't get back. I could place a winning bet that it wouldn't take long for them to figure out I was the girl who jumped on the bus with her.

I was in trouble. But more than that, we—me and Yrena—were in trouble together.

And honestly, I didn't care about me. All I wanted was for her to be okay.

Night Birds

We headed into the subway and went deeper downtown.

"Which way?" I asked once we emerged. Geographically I was all twisted up.

"Twin Towers mean downtown, Empire State means uptown," Callisto said as she pointed out the buildings.

"Now I know where I am on the planet—and that is a good feeling," I said.

Caitlin looped one arm through mine and Callisto took the other. Maurice followed us as we walked to Night Birds.

"It looks like a hole," Maurice said when we got there.

"Well, it is," Callisto said.

I didn't care what kind of a place it was as long as Yrena was inside of it.

Maurice opened the door and held it open for us. No one had ever done this for me before, not even my dad.

Callisto gave him a hard look.

"First the taxi, now here," Callisto said.

"Oh crap," he said. "I'm sorry. I know. I know. I shouldn't hold the door open for you ladies. You can do it yourselves and all that. My mom just drilled it into me that I should!"

"I don't mind," I said.

He held the door open for us and it wasn't in a weird anti-feminist way. It was in a genuinely thoughtful way.

"Me neither," Caitlin said.

"Well, I do," Callisto said.

"Well, how about on the way out, I let you hold the door open for me?" he said.

"All right," Callisto said. "That sounds fair. I'm your equal, you know. Rose and Caitlin are, too. "

"I know," Maurice said. "I'm sorry."

"You'd better be," Callisto said. "And we forgive you."

On the one hand, I didn't care if Maurice held open a door for me or not. I was happy either way and I didn't think it was that big a deal. But I saw Callisto's point and I wanted to support her because I didn't want to not be standing up for women. My conclusion was that negotiating a friendship is hard. Maybe that was why I had shied away from doing it.

"There she is!" Caitlin yelled.

I was so relieved to see Yrena sitting with Free in the back corner near the jukebox. Free waved us over, but Yrena turned away when she saw me.

I was here for Yrena. I had to figure out how to get Yrena to go home with me even if she wanted to hate me.

First, I tried the direct approach.

"Yrena, we gotta go," I said as soon as I got up to her. I even put my hand on her shoulder to convey a sense of urgency. Maurice, Caitlin, and Callisto sat and poured themselves glasses from Free's pitcher of beer.

"Why don't you sit down?" Callisto said. Then she waved to the empty seat at the table, like I had to hurry up before someone else took it.

"But I'm not staying," I told her. "Come on, Yrena."

"Sit down," Free said. "Or you'll ruin everything."

Then I got it.

If I kept standing up, I would draw attention to us because we were all in high school, and if the bartenders paid too close attention to us, they would know we weren't eighteen yet and everyone would get carded and kicked out or banned from here and it would all be my fault.

So I sat down.

That made Yrena relax.

"Beer?" Free asked, offering me the pitcher.

"No, thanks," I said.

There was a lot of food on the table. French fries. Buffalo wings. Nachos. All half-eaten. Like an American sampler plate.

Yrena was sipping on a glass of ice water, smiling at Free.

I looked at the plate of nachos in front of her and I immediately saw what she was doing. She hadn't really eaten any of the food she had in front of her. She had just pushed the chips and cheese around and made it look like she'd eaten some. I wondered if maybe she thought nachos were gross. I wondered if they had Mexican food in Russia. Had she ever seen chips, salsa, and melted cheese? Maybe she thought it was weird-looking.

I watched as she talked to everyone. It was kind of interesting the way she made herself amenable to people. She just participated while totally staying true to herself. She didn't want to eat the nachos because either she didn't like them or she was on a diet.

It didn't matter. The effort made everyone around her feel good.

I didn't have that gift.

"Rose, I want to stay a little while longer," she said to me.

"Love Potion No. 9" was playing on the jukebox. Isn't that funny, how you can remember something specific and insignificant like that? Now, whenever that song comes on, I remember that night.

"I'm not going home. I don't want this evening to end yet," Yrena told me.

"It's late," I pointed out. "I'm going to get in trouble. *You're* going to get in trouble."

"We are already in trouble—what will another few hours change?"

"Yrena wants to go to the protest," Free said. "How cool is that?"

And then he took her hand in his and held it.

I pushed my chair back so hard that it squeaked. I didn't know what to do, so I stood back up and went to the jukebox.

"I've got some quarters," Maurice said, joining me there.

"I'll help you. I want to make sure there is good music," Callisto said.

I flipped through the choices and tried to think of what I should do next.

"Oh, put on 'To Sir, with Love,'" Maurice said, giving me some quarters.

Callisto pressed the right buttons and I watched as the arm plucked out the correct 45 and played it.

Yrena came over and joined us.

"You are angry with me," she said.

"You left me," I said. "We were there together. I thought we were friends."

Maurice put the quarters in my hand and he and Callisto went back to the table to give us some space.

"We *are* friends," Yrena said.

"Friends don't do that to friends," I told her. Then I bit my tongue. I sounded just like Daisy.

"I want to see more things," Yrena said. "I want to go home tomorrow, after the Central Park protest."

"We have to go home now," I said.

I should have said that Todd had told me that there were suits at her house. Maybe that would have scared her. Or

125

maybe it wouldn't have. She probably already knew that there were suits there.

"I am not likely to come here again," she said.

"So what? Ask your parents to take you downtown. Ask them to take you to the protest."

Yrena shook her head. "You do not understand."

"No, I don't," I said. But I did understand a little bit. All I had to think about was the fact that we had climbed out of my window and escaped men who were watching us eat ice cream.

Yrena went back and sat down with Free.

I looked over at Callisto, who was shoving some nachos in her mouth. She was looking over at me. She punched Maurice in the shoulder; he pretended to be hurt, and then they both came back and joined me.

"I think Yrena is really sad," Maurice said.

"She is really stressing me out," I countered, giving him back his quarters.

"What's the big deal?" Callisto asked. "She's kind of a wet noodle. Let's give her cab fare and forget about her."

"If I lose Yrena again, I am afraid the KGB might come looking for me."

Maurice and Callisto looked at me blankly for a minute and then they burst out laughing. Maurice laughed into his closed fist, like I'd surprised him in a delightful way. Then he slapped my back like I was a buddy. Callisto pointed at me and laughed, like I was trying to get one over on her. They thought it was a joke—and maybe they were right. The whole thing was ridiculous.

"That's a good one, Rose. You. Are. Funny," Maurice said.

I was livid. Why had I ever agreed to come into Manhattan with a Russian girl I didn't even know? It was not worth all the headaches it was bringing me.

"Just give her a minute and try again," Maurice said.

"You're nicer than me," Callisto said, staring at Maurice. Really staring at him.

"What are you looking at?" he asked.

"Your face," Callisto said. "You know, you're cute? I don't think I've ever noticed how cute you are."

"Well, you're scary-looking," he said. "I mean, you look like David Bowie. You look just like a boy!"

"This coming from the son of Khadira!" Callisto said. "Drag queens do impersonations of your mom!"

"I know that," Maurice said. "That's a *good* thing. She's iconic."

"Well, David Bowie is iconic and he's androgynous. Are you afraid? Maybe you like boys. No shame in that."

"I'm not gay! Why does everyone always assume that a male ballet dancer is gay?"

"'Cause a lot of them are?" I said.

"Right," Maurice said. "I just—never mind, this is going to sound crazy. Forget it."

"No, just say it," Callisto said. "We're all friends here."

I didn't want to correct her.

"Well, it seems like a lot of girls throw themselves at me," Maurice said.

"I'm *not* throwing myself at you," Callisto said.

"Neither am I," I said.

"Well, I know that," Maurice said.

"Maybe girls throw themselves at you because you are one of the only straight boys in dance class?" I said.

"Maybe," Maurice said. "Or maybe it's that girls just want to be with me because my mom is famous."

"Is that hard?" Callisto asked. "Having Khadira be your mom?"

"It's confusing that everyone reacts to who my mom is, you know? It doesn't have anything to do with me. So I just want to take my time. Sort things out. Meet someone I like first."

"I respect that," Callisto said. "Our dad is Stone Mazzeretti."

"Who's that?" Maurice asked.

Judging from Callisto's reaction, this wasn't exactly the right answer. I was glad Maurice had asked and not me.

"He's a famous jazz musician," Callisto explained. "A trumpet player."

"So you get it," Maurice said.

"Yeah, it might be smaller than Khadira, but I get it."

Maurice looked relieved.

"Thanks for not laughing at me," he said.

"It's no laughing matter," Callisto said. "And I wouldn't laugh at you, anyway."

Wait, I thought. *Where is Callisto going with this flirting?*

Before I could figure it out, someone started yelling, "No. No. NO!"

"Caleb!" Caitlin yelled back from the table.

And then Caleb was standing in front of us.

"What are you guys doing here? Are you following me?" He looked like he was scowling again, but not his eyes. They were shining brightly and playfully as they took me in, like he was trying to decide if I was more than a kind of thorn.

"More like are *you* following *us*," Callisto pointed out.

"This is a drama department hangout," he said. "Don't you have places that you can go?"

"Do you always have to be such a jerk?" Callisto shot back.

"You'd better be buying the beer," Caleb said. "And then I'll forgive you."

"Jerk."

"Come and join us, Caleb," Caitlin said from the table.

Caleb and Callisto both laughed and then did a special handshake that they only did with each other and with Caitlin. It was a triplet thing.

"Hey, you. Underwear girl," Caleb said as we all went back to the table and sat down.

He shook the longish, bangy part of his hair out of his eyes and stared at me. His mouth was actually ajar.

"Who are you again?" he asked.

He scratched the scruff on his cheek and cocked his head sideways.

"Rose," I said.

"Are you really wearing underwear?" he asked.

I blushed a little.

"It's long underwear," I said. "I didn't know I was coming out."

"Crap. It's almost midnight," Free said, looking at his watch. "I have to go home. Curfew!"

"And we should go soon so we don't have to wait forever for a ferry," Caitlin said to her brother and sister.

And just like that, everyone was dumping all of their cash onto the table and heading outside.

"Wait," Yrena said. "I have not picked a song yet."

She took a quarter off the pile of money on the table and came over to the jukebox.

"I think we have time for one more song, yes?" she asked impishly. She had a mischievous look on her face, like she was up to a kind of fun that we would all be really missing out on if we didn't stay to hear what the song would be.

"One more song," I said.

She put her quarter in the jukebox. She didn't even flip through the pages to see what was on there; she just looked down at the big red buttons and pressed them randomly, like she could somehow channel the perfect song.

We all waited to see what would come up. To see what kind of tone chance would let us end the night on.

The needle fell on the groove . . . and there it was.

The bass line came on.

Bam. Bam. Bam. Bam.

Super Freak.

Yrena bent her elbows, stuck them out, and began to strut. Maurice did a little twitch move with his shoulder. I started to tap my foot. Callisto cocked her head from side to side. Caitlin moved the table to make some room.

And then there was the bumping of butts. And bodies sliding side to side. And dancers pointing to each other, giving cues.

Superfreakyyyyyowwwwww.

We were leading the disco on the bar floor, drawing attention to ourselves. People at the other tables began to clap and encourage us. We got more freaky.

Free had the best moves. He didn't have ballet stuck on him, so he was all moves and gyrating hips. We let him take the center of our dance circle. He knew all the words and he serenaded us all as he grabbed Yrena and drew her toward him. She laughed and laughed, right from her belly. Right from her heart.

And then, just as suddenly as it had begun, the needle

lifted up off the 45 and the song was over. But we still had the moves inside of us as we made our way to the door and spilled out onto Second Avenue.

Dancing had made us all a little closer. We didn't want to let go of the beat. It was like the music was still inside of us, keeping us together. Like we all wanted to see if there was maybe one more moment that would shake out of us, that we could all linger over.

But Yrena didn't ask for another moment.

She said her big good-byes to everyone. It was like she was saying good-bye to her nearest and dearest friends, and she didn't even know them.

I watched her, and what I remember noticing was her hair. When we had left the Bronx earlier that evening, it had been in a high, tight bun. Now her hair was in a high pony-tail. Was she coming undone? Was she letting the inner her shine out for one day?

"So, I'll see you at the march tomorrow?" Free said.

"Yes," Yrena promised.

"I'm not so sure about that," I said, imagining what she would face if the suits were really hanging outside of her house when she got home.

"Yes." Yrena said it to Free, but she was looking at me.

Yrena and Free were hovering around each other. I could tell she liked him. I looked at him and didn't see anything so special. He was big. He had a beard. His shoulders were very large. He looked like a football player masquerading as a hippie. He was normal-looking. I didn't think that anything about Free was hot at all. He was an average American guy.

Oh, right, I thought. *Average. American. Guy.* Poor Todd. He never really stood a chance with her. He was too eccentric.

Free kind of did the pin on Yrena as she leaned up against the gate that covered the window of the store next door to Night Birds.

I watched as he put his forehead close to Yrena and kind of leaned into her, like he might like Yrena, too. It was sweet. And weird. But I noticed that about Free. He might look like he could be on a football team or date a cheerleader, but he had eyes that cared. I bet that was why he wore the hippie clothes and the beard. He was trying to distance himself from who he thought the world thought he should be.

Were we all like that? Were we all trying to change how we looked on the outside to match how we felt on the inside? Were we all trying to change how people saw us? I knew it annoyed me that Daisy and the Science girls wore leg warmers and headbands when they didn't even dance. And I wanted so badly for the world to see me as a dancer, as something that was not like my brother in full nerd regalia, something not like my parents in their business power suits. I wanted people to look at our family portrait and see that I did not belong to them. That I was an alien. That I was different.

"So, I'll see you tomorrow then, Yrena?" Free said Yrena's name like my brother did, like it was a piece of music. "I'll be near the big tree on the right side of the Great Lawn."

"Good-bye," she said.

"Good-bye," he echoed, and then, with one last glance back at her, walked away.

Yrena watched him go and looked so sad.

"I should call my brother and let him know we're on our way," I said, reaching for the nearest pay phone.

"I can take you guys back uptown," Maurice said.

"They don't need a boy to protect them," Callisto said.

I slid the dime into the slot and dialed.

"I'm not saying they do. And I'm not saying I can protect them. I'm just saying my mom is out of town and I have the time."

"Where's your mom?" Callisto asked.

The phone was ringing.

"Rose?" It was Todd. "Did you find her?"

"Yeah."

"Thank God. There is some weird shit going on next door."

"What do you mean?"

"I don't want to say—I'm worried they've tapped our phones."

"Don't be paranoid," I said.

"The suits were upstairs talking to Mom and Dad. Wait—did you hear that?"

I wanted to say that Todd was acting crazy, but I had heard a click.

I freaked out and hung up the phone. I should have called back, but instead I comforted myself with the thought that at least Todd knew that I had found her. I rejoined the group.

"She's in Los Angeles, shooting a guest spot on the show *The Nemesis*," Maurice said.

"Our parents are upstate," Callisto said.

"I hate being left alone," Maurice said.

"We can walk you guys to the subway," Caleb volunteered.

"We're going there, too. Only in the other direction," Callisto said.

You would have had to have been in a coma not to see that I was struggling with something. But how could I tell everyone about the click on the phone? It seemed so ridiculous. They didn't believe me about the KGB.

Maybe I *was* making it all up.

Sometimes, when people can sense that you are upset and not talking, they know that you are really upset, and sometimes what it means is that they'll start acting nice. Extra nice. Which is how everyone was acting toward me. Even Caleb, the jerk. He was making small talk that I wasn't really listening to as his steps fell in time with mine.

". . . saw Pacino in *American Buffalo* last year . . ."

". . . I have an Atari . . ."

". . . pretty good at *Asteroids* . . ."

". . . I play music, too . . ."

Yrena stepped in between us, put her arm around my shoulder, and pulled me away from him.

"I'm sorry," she said.

"I'm sorry, too," I said.

"We are friends, right?"

"Yeah." It was funny to think that by that time, it was true.

"Then I can tell you a secret," she said.

"Yes, of course," I said.

I figured that she would tell me that she had gone to second base with Free. Or that she had gotten a little tipsy.

"I leave for Moscow next week," she said. "We are moving back. That is why I do not want to go home. I do not want to let this evening go."

Once I had a bucket of ice water thrown on me. It made me feel numb and wet and it was as though my skin had been stung with a million tiny needles. That was how I felt when Yrena said that she was moving back to Russia. I wanted to pretend that she hadn't said it. Like maybe we could just move on to another subject.

"No way—you're going back to Moscow?" Callisto jumped in, holding her clove cigarette between her thumb and her forefinger and flicking the stub out into the street. "That's cool."

"I will never be in New York City again," Yrena said. "This is my night."

"Whoa, that sucks," Caleb said.

"Why didn't you tell me sooner?" I asked.

"I was afraid," she said. "Once we got on the bus, I was afraid that if I told you, we would go back. I just wanted to see New York. I'm sorry."

"So that's it?" Callisto said.

"It seems weird now that we've met you that you're leaving forever," Caitlin said.

"We just spent the whole night looking for you," Callisto added.

"I know, I know," Yrena said. "I was selfish."

She put her face in her hands.

"We have to go home," I said. "I'm sorry."

But I didn't want her to leave.

"We could all ride with you guys uptown," Callisto said. I noticed she was looking at Maurice when she said it.

"No," Caleb said. "Look, I feel for you. You're going back to the Soviet Union. But I don't want to take a train to the Bronx."

"Caleb, stop being an ass," Caitlin said.

"I have to get up early to go to the march tomorrow." Caleb shook his hair out of his eyes. He was scowling again. I could see that he was trying to work something out. "It seems to me like everything that protest is trying to accomplish is happening right here. Right now. This is how world peace starts. We shouldn't have to separate right now. We should

137

get closer. They tell us that we couldn't possibly get along. Well, look at us. We're getting along just fine, if you ask me."

He was right to look pissed off. To be brooding over something. To be pointing out the obvious.

"You know," he said, "I'd go with you if you were taking her sightseeing or something."

I looked at Caleb. He didn't seem so jerky anymore. He seemed like someone who understood that this situation really sucked.

"Can we go to the Statue of Liberty?" Yrena asked.

"You can't go to the Statue of Liberty—the island is closed at night," Callisto told her.

"But you *could* go on the Staten Island Ferry and kind of see everything," Caleb said—and he would know, because that was where he and the other Cs lived. "And then we could go home."

"We have to go home," I said. "The suits . . ."

"Yes," Yrena said. "I know."

She put her hand on my shoulder to quiet me, as though if I kept saying it out loud, the suits would come running around the corner. But they didn't know where we were. In a way, we were safe from them as long as we stayed downtown.

We were almost at the subway station. Callisto, Caitlin, and Maurice were insisting on escorting us uptown.

"Come on," I said to Caleb. "You know you want to be

our bodyguard. Maybe you can disarm muggers with your performance art."

"Are you saying that at our rehearsal we were that bad?" Caleb said.

"No, I thought it was good." I grinned. "I just mean that you'd probably have the element of surprise."

"Right," he said. "Bamboozle them with absurdist art forms."

For a split second, his perma-scowl melted away.

"Fine," he grumbled, going back to his normal, angsty self. "How could anyone resist such a charming compliment?"

Before we went underground, Yrena's eyes swept one big, long look around the city. She sighed. She touched her heart. She blew kisses to the north, south, east, and west.

I hung back a bit and took a slight pause to try to see the beauty that she always seemed to see. Now, looking back over my shoulder as we descended into the subway, I saw it, too. Oh, the buildings in New York. Oh, the city that never sleeps. Oh, the great wonder of a city that never slept.

New York. So beautiful.

Clamshell

I tried to think about the ways we could sneak back into our houses. Which was funny, because I figured that most people my age tried to figure out ways to sneak *out* of their houses.

The things I was thinking about were crazy.

Like that it was true that we would be in just as much trouble tomorrow as we would be if we went home tonight.

It was weighing heavily on me that Yrena was going back to Moscow next week.

It was just past midnight and the subway car was empty except for some tired man in the corner. He was eyeballing us while he tried to sleep. I was guessing that he just wanted to make sure that we were not the kind of kids who were going to cause any trouble.

Caleb was sitting really close next to me. His leg was pressed up against mine. He didn't seem to be giving it any thought, though. That was my department, to overthink things.

I kept stealing glances at him. I kept finding things to like in his face. His lips. His cheekbone. His nostril.

While I was sitting with my legs crossed like a lady, Yrena was swinging on the poles in the car.

She lifted her legs in impossible ways.

Yrena was doing a private dance performance, street theater with us as an audience. Maurice shouted out combination moves to Yrena, who incorporated them into her improv. She mixed it up pretty well, too. I noticed that the guy in the corner kept one eye open and was smiling. Yrena noticed, too, because when she was done she did an exaggerated bow. I noticed that the guy had a veteran's pin on. He was youngish, so it must have been Vietnam. I bet he didn't know that she was his enemy. He actually clapped as he got off at Times Square.

A bunch of people got on then, too, including some cops. I motioned to Yrena to stop. She plopped down across from me. Her face was flushed. Her eyes were flashing.

Her eyes.

They took everything in. I felt like I always had this measured wariness about me when I was on the subway, this New-York-don't-mess-with-me look, but Yrena was so fresh-faced and eager. I tried it on. I looked with excited eyes. I *squinted*. Everything went kind of pink. Or yellow-y. It was nice.

"Oh!" Yrena said, tugging at me as the car pulled into the 66th Street station. "Look! Lincoln Center!"

We were just a block away from the epicenter of New York City dance, theater, music, and opera.

"I would have loved to see Makarova dance," Yrena went on. "I am going to go to the school that trained her when I get back. The Vaganova school."

"I saw Suzanne Farrell a few weeks ago," Maurice said.

"Oh! Suzanne Farrell!" Yrena said. "Was she dancing with d'Amboise?"

"Yeah," Maurice said. "And what about Baryshnikov? Have you seen him?"

"Ach," she said. "Baryshnikov is not so special."

And then we all laughed because we all knew she was lying. We knew Baryshnikov was nothing to sneer at. We knew she was making a joke. Or maybe she had to say it. Maybe once you defected, you were proclaimed to be "not so special."

Just as the bell rang to signal that the doors were about to close, I did something a little crazy. I jumped up and held them until the conductor had to open the doors again.

"Hey, you. Kid," one of the cops said, starting to come up to me. "Don't do that."

But the doors were open now, and Maurice, Caleb, Caitlin, Callisto, and Yrena knew that the plan had changed and that I was now in charge. They followed me and we all went flying out the door together like a flock of birds. The doors closed and there we were on the platform, breathless and flushed. The train was leaving without us.

Then the new me's resolve, with the new idea, faltered.

"What am I doing?" I groaned.

"You are being the most awesome American hostess to our friend Yrena on her last free night in the U.S. of A.," Caitlin said, putting her arm around my shoulder and giving me an encouraging lift.

That made me smile, because I liked that she thought I'd done something cool.

"All I know is that a girl like Yrena can't have lived in New York City for two years and never have seen Lincoln Center," Maurice said.

"That would be a *crime*. I mean, if the shoe were on the other foot, I would want to go see the Kirov ballet, and I don't even like ballet," Callisto said.

"Or the Bolshoi!" Yrena said.

"Or if I couldn't see them, I would want to at least see the building where they danced," Caitlin said.

"Come on!" Caleb said. "Enough yapping. More moving along." He led the way through the turnstile and up the stairs. We emerged on Broadway and it was dark and empty—and yet, as always, there was the bustle of the city. The taxis going here and there. People still walking around. But mostly it was empty. Mostly the city seemed like it was ours.

"It's always alive, this city," Yrena said. "That is what makes it beautiful."

We walked toward the white marble of Lincoln Center. It never ceased to make me excited, seeing those three buildings and that fountain. I wanted to dance on those stages so badly that I could taste it.

"I am still crushed that I wasn't accepted into the School of American Ballet," Maurice said. "I have the wrong body type."

"Yrena probably would have gotten in. She's got the perfect Balanchine ballet body," I said. "Tiny head, short torso, very long, lean legs, and delicate arms."

We let Yrena run in front of us. She ran up the stairs and did leaps around the fountain.

"Oh, it is beautiful," she said.

I was one hundred percent awake, because it was actually physically impossible to be exhausted or mad or cranky or frightened or freaked out when there was someone who was so happy in front of me. I just had to go with it.

"All right," Yrena said. "I have seen it. Thank you. I am ready to go home."

I could see that she had resigned herself to the fact that after this we were going back to the Bronx and that our American Night Out adventure was over.

But I wanted one more minute. I got that feeling. That feeling of how unfair everything in the world was.

I kicked the side of the fountain.

How dumb was it that Yrena had lived next door to me for two years, and because we were strangers, with governments that were enemies, we had never before taken a chance to say hello? A few hours together and it was obvious what we had missed out on. Even though we had been taught to fear, there was nothing to be afraid of.

Here we were, just a bunch of kids hanging out in America, getting along perfectly fine with no hint of discontent between us. And if we had been hanging out in front of the Kremlin, we'd have been just as happy and gotten along just as well.

We were warm. I wasn't going to let the cold win.

"No. Wait. I want to show you something else," I said.

Museums.

Central Park.

The Twin Towers.

The UN.

Coney Island.

The Statue of Liberty.

Lincoln Center.

Dancing.

I led us back behind the State Theater, over to the Clamshell. Whenever there was an outdoor performance, they would set up folding chairs. But now it was just an empty space with an open stage.

"Look," I said. "Here's your chance to perform at Lincoln Center."

Yrena took a second. Then she carefully took off her sweater, dug into her bag, got something out, and then handed me the bag to hold. She made her way up to the stage. She sat on the stairs and pulled off her shoes and put

145

on Gelsey Kirkland's toe shoes—the ones from my room. They were her same size.

It didn't even bother me that she had stolen something from my room. If I had thought about it, I would have given her a pair as a souvenir.

She was wearing regular clothes, but when she stood center stage and took a position for an adagio, she looked like a swan.

She stood perfectly still. She took it in. And then she was off. She began to dance and twirl and leap and do magic. She twisted and sighed and I noticed that I was feeling a bit jealous—not of her foot technique, since mine was good, too. But her arms. Her arms were near perfect. After each fluid movement, they always fell into perfect place.

Callisto, Caitlin, and Caleb followed her lead. They took their hands and they clapped and slapped the stage, making a rhythm. They began to play in time to her dancing.

I was breathless.

And then she was done.

Why on earth would she want to quit if she could dance like that? I would never understand that. It made me want to dance *more*.

Maurice and I began to clap and throw fake flowers. Yrena curtsied deeply and pretended to gather the flowers in her hands, blowing kisses at the invisible-except-for-me-and-Maurice audience.

Then she waved us both over.

Maurice and I went straight to the stage, like we'd been hypnotized by the moment, by Yrena and her beautiful arms. We climbed up to her and she put her imaginary flowers down and she slid her arms around our waists, pulling us into an embrace. And then we peeled away and we all began to dance. Together.

And as we were dancing, Caleb, Caitlin, and Callisto began to use their voices to add to the percussion. It sounded eerie and ghostly and it blended in with the sounds of the city. It made for an arresting and haunting sound track. I was dancing. I was the stars and the moon and the sky. I was air.

I had been bitten by the evening and my heart went straight to my feet. I could feel it. I could feel myself being carried on the waves of music coming from Caitlin, Callisto, and Caleb. I could feel a string pulling me, Yrena, and Maurice together and apart.

My body was a complex equation. X was my soul. Y was Yrena. Sometimes Maurice divided or bisected us. I looped and bent and leapt, and when I came together in sync on a landing with Yrena, something from that point on was different in me. I just moved. I poured myself into the moment. Fluid. Silent. Wordless. And Yrena was always there, receiving and reflecting everything I sent toward her. She matched me and I matched her. There was a selfish beauty to dancing alone, but when you opened up your heart and let it flow out to others, it seemed that for a brief moment you could share a

147

soul. I did not need to think about where I would go next. Every step, bend, jump, and glide felt perfect.

We, all of us, three dancers, a musician, and an actor, came to a stop at the same moment, ending on the mournful note of Caitlin's voice.

I had to remind myself that we were going home and that Yrena would be in the Soviet Union in a few days. I was blinking back tears because it was such an unfairly transcendent moment. I didn't want it to end. I was afraid that I might not ever dance this freely or this well again.

"I am going to quit dancing," Yrena said. "I don't need to do it anymore."

There was something so final in what she said. But there was no remorse. It was Yrena speaking her truth. She had such a gift, but what was the point of the gift if you did not have the passion?

I felt as though I was finally awake as a person. It was like I had just been born.

And I knew what the first step would be.

"Let's go to that march tomorrow," I said.

"But we cannot. My parents won't let me go out once I get home," Yrena said.

"So then I guess we can't go back home yet," I said.

Maybe I was wrong. Maybe I should've gotten us home. But I didn't.

I pointed us toward adventure.

The City Never Sleeps

"Okay, what's the plan?" Caleb asked, rubbing his hands together with glee.

"The plan is to do everything," I told him.

"We should definitely go to our house," Caitlin said.

Caleb nodded. "Yeah, if only because taking the Staten Island Ferry is one of the best ways to see New York City."

"Yeah! Come to Staten Island with us!" Callisto chimed in. "Spend the night at our house. Our parents are out of town."

"Spend the night?" Yrena asked.

"Yeah, sleep over," Caitlin said.

"Sleep over," Yrena said dreamily. Callisto was nodding her head up and down: Yes. Yes. Yes. "Then we can go to the march tomorrow?"

"Can I come, too?" Maurice asked. "No one is at my house, and if I go back home now, I might oversleep."

"Sure," Callisto said before he was even finished.

"So where should we start?" Caleb asked.

"What about starting there?!" Maurice was pointing at a hot-dog cart, and we all agreed that Yrena needed to try one of everything. Hot dog. Pretzel. Warm chestnuts.

We were walking and Yrena was making faces as she tasted the different street foods. We stepped past Columbus Circle.

"Where are we going?" Caitlin asked.

"How do you get to Carnegie Hall?" I asked.

"Practice," Callisto said.

"Ha, ha," Caitlin said.

"Let's go by it and then head over to Fifth Avenue and look at the windows," I said.

It was too bad that it wasn't Christmastime. The window displays were something that I loved as a kid and I would have liked to share them with Yrena. But I was certain that the October window displays would be just as interesting to her.

"You girls are a lot different from what I thought you were like at school," Maurice said.

I almost told him that I was probably *exactly* the way that he thought I was at school. Right now this was me being different. I was not myself right now. And I was enjoying it.

"Why do you always kind of hang back in class, Rose? You're not that bad a dancer."

"Thanks a lot," I said. I knew where I stood in class. I didn't want it pointed out to me.

"It's not like you couldn't be better—it's just, you always come late. You're not warmed-up properly. You concentrate so hard that you don't feel it in your body. I can see that in class. So you just sort of do the minimum. That gets you by, but I think you could probably stand out in a better way."

"But not great," I said. "I could never be great. Like you. Or Yrena. Why bother trying if I'm not going to ever be great?"

"Not everyone is going to be great," Maurice said. "And besides, none of us know what we are yet and that doesn't mean you can't be better than you are now by trying. I saw you up there with me and Yrena. You got it then."

I was feeling exposed and vulnerable. I didn't want to cry in front of Maurice on the first day of our maybe-friendship just because he was right that I didn't try hard enough in dance class.

So I did something I never did.

I let it *slide*.

Caleb fell into pace with me but we didn't say anything.

I almost thought we were breathing in and out at the same time. I wanted to ask him if he felt as I did, that something had happened to all of us on that stage, because there was an electricity between us. Like we were a unit. Like there was a thread between us.

"Wait," Yrena said from up ahead. "What is this?" Then she stopped so short that Caleb and I nearly knocked into her.

Yrena was at a dead stop in front of an elaborate-looking doorway.

"Look, Russian bears!" she said.

The Russian Tea Room.

"Oh, I've heard of this place," Caitlin said.

"This is a fancy place. Really fancy," Callisto added.

"That's right!" Yrena said. "I have been telling you, Russia is fancy."

"But this is expensive fancy," Caitlin said.

"Besides, it's closed," Caleb said. "It's after one A.M."

Yrena stepped up to the glass doors and peered inside. Then she began to knock.

"What are you doing?" I asked.

"Someone is in there," she said. "I can see a light and people moving around."

She knocked on the window a bit harder. Then she pulled her hair out of her ponytail and let it fall softly around her shoulders.

An older blond woman opened the door, and she and Yrena began to speak in Russian. The woman looked us all over and then opened the door up a bit farther and let us in.

When we walked in, Yrena seemed lighter on her feet.

"You all have shown me New York City," she said. "I want to show you a little bit of Russia!"

Even though the place was clearly closed, there were still people sitting at tables. It was the post-theater crowd. Not the audience, but the *performers.*

"Isn't that Betty Buckley and the cast of *Cats?*" Maurice whispered.

"Yeah," I said.

"Look, that's Athol Fugard," Caleb said. "God. I loved *Master Harold and the Boys*."

It was hard not to stare at them or at the decor. It was a restaurant that looked stuck in time—it was 1982, and yet in here it felt like it was the 1930s. Everyone's eyes were as big as saucers as they took in all the gold and brocade.

"This place is crazy," Callisto said.

"It smells all kinds of good in here," Maurice said.

"Whatever it is they have cooking, it has to be delicious," Caitlin said.

Maurice pointed at a picture of Nureyev in tights, doing an arabesque, his face serious and magnificent, his extension exquisite. Nureyev was looking right out of the frame, right at us from there on the wall, welcoming us.

Yrena was speaking to the blond woman again, and now instead of looking surly, the woman was laughing.

"What'd she say?" Caitlin asked.

"She says that she will take care of us."

The hostess signaled one of the waiters and spoke in Russian to him. The waiter nodded and smiled and brought us to a nice cozy booth in the back. He pulled the table out to let us all in and then slid the table back. We were completely hemmed in—no chance to dine and ditch from here. I sank deep into the lush seat.

It felt good to sit down. My muscles were tired. I knew tiredness and soreness from dancing, but this was different

153

somehow. It felt like world-weariness. Or weight-of-the-world-on-my-shoulders-ness. I closed my eyes for just a second. I was just resting.

"You okay?" Caleb asked. Somehow he'd managed to get next to me again.

"Tired," I said. "Worried."

The waiter brought us ice water for the table, but no menus. Yrena hadn't been lying when she'd said that they'd take care of us. When the waiter came back, it was with an ornate silver pot of coffee, which he poured into china cups for each of us. It was the most delicious coffee I'd ever tasted.

"Are you really quitting?" I asked.

"Yes," Yrena said. "I will go home tomorrow and while I am facing my punishment, I will take the chance to tell them how I really feel."

"How do you feel when you dance?" Maurice asked.

"As though I am a puppet," Yrena said. "Or a show dog."

"Sometimes I feel as though my body isn't my own," Maurice said. "But I never feel like a puppet."

"I feel as though each muscle, each point that I hit, is like some complicated math problem that my body has to solve," I said. "I love that. When I solve it, it's as though the universe sings."

"On the days where I let myself, yes," Yrena said. "I have felt like that. I will miss those moments. But not the rest of it."

"That's how I feel about music," Caleb said. "That's why I went into the drama department."

"When I dance, I feel as though my heart is bigger than my body," I said. "And that I am giving it back to everyone who is alive."

"You should dance like that in class," Maurice said. "Why don't you?"

"I don't know," I said. "I freeze up. I get scared."

"I saw you tonight," Caleb said. "I don't know that much about dance, but I know that you don't have anything to be scared of."

The waiter came back and put down a bunch of plates and some bowls of ice with tiny bowls of stuff inside of them — egg whites, egg yellows, onions.

"Ew. What is it?" Callisto asked.

"Russian delicacies!" Yrena proclaimed. "Caviar. Blintzes. So delicious."

"Caviar — fish eggs," Caleb said. "Yum."

But I could tell that he meant *Yuck*.

"You've never had caviar before, Caleb!" Caitlin said.

"Sure I have. Well, not this kind, but the orange kind."

"Mmm. It's good," Callisto said.

"Salty," Maurice said.

"Fish eggs," Caitlin said.

"Delicious," I said.

Caleb tried some with a pinched nose, but then he went back for more.

"There is a part of me that wants to stay here in this big city," Yrena said as we all dug in and stuffed our faces. "Is it bad for me to say that there is a part of me that does not want to go home?"

"Do you want to defect?" Caleb whispered.

Yrena shook her head. "No. But I also want to know this place. I want to know you. I want to be able to be myself."

"I don't know how a person does that," I said.

"Now, knowing you, there is a part of me that sees a different path. A different way that I could be if I were American." Yrena sighed and lifted the coffee cup to her mouth.

"Maybe things will change one day?" I said.

She shook her head.

But, I realized, that was what *I* wanted.

Change.

The waiter cleared our plates and dropped something on the table.

My heart sank because I thought it was a bill. But then I noticed that it was a piece of paper.

"What's that?" I asked.

"The price for the meal," Yrena said. "I am going to visit and bring news to his grandmother in Moscow. That's her address."

She slipped the piece of paper into her shoe.

"For safekeeping," she said.

Staten Island Ferry

After window-shopping on Fifth Avenue, running on the steps at St. Patrick's Cathedral, looking at Rockefeller Center, and jetting over to Times Square, we hopped on the train and got ourselves to the Whitehall Street/South Ferry station to catch the Staten Island Ferry.

I felt giddy. We all did.

We had to move to make the ferry. We didn't want to wait for the next one. We ran. All of us. Running and leaping. Leaping and running. We laughed as we jumped onto the deck just as the man was about to put the chain up.

It was after two A.M. and New York City was moving away from us at a slow pace. The city shone. It glowed. It winked at us. We were standing at the back of the Staten Island Ferry so we could best see everything.

We didn't have to say anything to each other, and I liked that.

"It's cold," I said. "It'll be winter soon."

"You do not know what winter is," Yrena said. "Your winters here are not cold."

"They feel cold to me," I said.

She was the only one of us who didn't look like she could use an extra sweater.

Maurice and Callisto left together to get us all some hot chocolate from the concession stand.

Yrena, Caitlin, Caleb, and I stood side by side at the railing and stared at the city as it drifted away from us.

"I bet you don't have cities like this in the Soviet Union," Caleb said to Yrena.

"There are cities in Russia that are prettier than New York," Yrena replied.

Caleb shook his head. "That can't be true."

"It is," Yrena said matter-of-factly.

"No way!" Caleb said. "I mean, look at that!"

Caleb began to point out everything there was to see on the boat ride. He indicated what was obvious to anyone with half a brain, that New York City was, in fact, the best city in the world. He made motioning movements to lower Manhattan. Governor's Island. The Statue of Liberty. Ellis Island.

"It is very beautiful, but it is not for me," Yrena said. Still, I noticed that her eyes followed Caleb's every swoosh. Her face took in every new view.

"Let me ask you something," Caleb said. "Do you think your country is better than ours?"

"It is," Yrena said.

"How can you say that your way is better when you can't even leave the Bronx without sneaking out of it?" Caleb said. "I can do anything I want. I can go anywhere I want. I can say anything I want."

"Your department stores. Your supermarkets and delis. Your blue jeans," Yrena was mumbling to me.

"Yrena, you're wearing blue jeans!" I pointed out.

"Here is how we are different. Russians *feel* things. Russians feel the weight of history. Americans are all surface and plastic," Yrena said.

"I feel things," I said.

"Me, too," Caitlin said.

"Not like we do," Yrena said.

"You can't see into my heart," Caleb said.

Caleb was looking at me with an intensity that made me buzz. He was wired up, and that thing I felt growing between us just kept buzzing louder. I wanted to take his hand. I wanted to just take it and hold it and tell him that I loved the way he argued.

Instead, I looked away from him. I looked over at New Jersey while they continued to bicker. There were ships tugging along, too, container ships, moving toward the docks.

Maurice and Callisto rejoined us and distributed the hot chocolate. Maurice was being all upbeat and I noticed that he was also standing really close to Callisto. They were laughing and poking each other and it was obvious that somewhere between the Metropolitan Museum of Art and the Staten Island Ferry they had become a couple. They were so into their little world of getting to know each other that they were oblivious to the extra chill in the air from the silence that has settled onto me, Caitlin, Caleb, and Yrena.

"Oh, look at that," Maurice said, pointing out the Statue of Liberty.

Lady Liberty was a beautiful old thing. She stood there, metal torch all lit up and raised high, all green and lovely.

"Yrena," I said. "We can at least agree that that is just beautiful!"

"'Give me your tired, your poor, your huddled masses yearning to breathe free, the wretched refuse of your teeming shore. Send these, the homeless, tempest-tost to me, I lift my lamp beside the golden door!'" Caleb quoted.

There was something about the way that he closed his eyes as he said it. The way that his hand moved a bit in a wave, as though the words were a kind of music that he was singing. Caleb knew how to say something and make it seem majestic.

"'The wretched refuse'?" Yrena said. "Isn't 'refuse' garbage?"

"You are crazy!" Caleb said.

"That you take in the garbage from the world?" Yrena said, laughing.

"That's not what they mean, Yrena. Not *actual* garbage," I said.

160

"Yeah, what she said. Not *actual* garbage, Yrena. It's not like that," Caleb said. "It means that we are a refuge for all those who are oppressed. Like, we're good. We're a *haven*."

Yrena turned her head toward him and I saw her face soften from the hard lines that had been there since the conversation started.

"What do they call it? The American Dream? It seems as though America is the dream because America is dreaming. Not awake," Yrena said. "That is what my parents say."

"Wait. Maybe Yrena is right. Maybe we *are* the garbage collectors of the world," Caitlin said.

"You mean, maybe we are the wretched refuse?" Callisto asked.

"Well, you know what they say," Caleb said. "Beautiful gardens grow out of crap."

"And one man's garbage is another man's treasure," I said.

I thought about America and garbage. I stared out at the black inkiness of the Hudson River. My treasure. My garbage.

Why do we have to belong to any country at all? I wanted to stay on the ferry, floating on the water, neither here nor there. I didn't want to be part of the politics. I just wanted to be friends with whomever I wanted to be friends with. And everyone I wanted to be friends with was right here on the boat.

All Night Jam

The Mazzerettis' house was not too far from the ferry dock.

Their living room was filled with instruments. There were guitars everywhere on stands. A piano in the corner. Violin cases and flute cases and trumpet cases. A snare drum. Some bongos. There was hardly room for the television, the couch, and the La-Z-Boy.

As soon as we got inside, Caleb, Caitlin, and Callisto headed straight for the instruments.

"Start in C," Callisto said once her violin was at the ready. Caitlin was at the piano and Caleb was on the acoustic guitar.

Yrena, Maurice, and I sat down on the couch. They weren't putting on a show. It was more like a nighttime ritual, like warm milk or hot Sleepytime Tea. The Mazzerettis played music to unwind from a long day.

First they jammed. Then they started playing standards and singing together, with Caitlin taking the lead vocals and Caleb and Callisto throwing in an occasional harmony.

"Switch," Caitlin said to Caleb, reaching for the guitar.

"No, I want to play guitar," he protested.

"Don't be such a greedy guts," Callisto snapped back.

"Fine." He sat down at the piano, and Caitlin picked up the acoustic guitar and started strumming. "But let's play something that our guests can sing, too."

"Oh, I can't sing," I said.

"*Anyone* can sing," Callisto said.

We agreed on "Twinkle, Twinkle, Little Star." Maurice and I joined in, but Yrena was silent. She didn't know the words. When the song was done and we were trying to figure out another song to play, Yrena began to sing a Russian song a cappella. We sat there, transfixed—her voice was shaky, but that made it even more moving.

"*Spi, mladenec moj prekrasnyj . . .*"

The triplets listened and then figured out how to play some notes along with her. When she was done, she translated:

"*Sleep, my lovely baby, sleep.*

The clear moon quietly watches over you.

I will tell you fairy tales

And I will sing you songs.

Close your eyes and drift to sleep.

Sleep, my lovely baby, sleep."

We were there and we were safe and we were happy and we were singing. Everything in that room seemed right. As though the very molecules in the air had lined up correctly.

"Time for sleep," Callisto said as she put away her violin. Then she went over to Maurice and led him down the hall into her bedroom.

The rest of us looked at each other, not knowing what we should do.

"We three girls can bunk down in my parents' room," Caitlin said. "We can't go into my bedroom—it looks like it's now a love nest."

"Mom and Dad's room is the one room we can't make a mess of," Caleb said. "So I'm not sure it's the best place for a sleepover."

"Well, what are we supposed to do?" Caitlin asked.

I didn't care how they figured it out. I was still on the couch, so I lay down and I pulled the quilt that covered the back of it over me.

"I'm fine here," I said, closing my eyes.

As I drifted off, I heard Caitlin and Caleb arguing about who was going to sleep where. I didn't hear what was decided until a bit later when the couch moved and a hand slid under the small of my back.

"Don't worry, I'm not going to touch you or anything," Caleb was whispering.

"You *are* touching me," I said.

His hand was actually now on my butt. I knew he didn't mean it in a coming-on-to-me way, but it was still weird.

He looked embarrassed. Like he knew that he was touching my butt and there was not too much he could do about it.

"You're just sleeping on the guitar strap," he said. "And I kind of want to play some more."

I lifted my back up and he pulled his guitar and strap away.

"Where are Yrena and Caitlin?" I asked. I was sort of asleep and sort of awake.

"They're sleeping in my room, on my bed." His fingers pressed on the strings, which made a muted sound.

"In the same bed?" I asked. "I feel bad. Should I offer to switch?"

"I think they became instant friends."

"She's cool like that, isn't she?"

"Yeah, if they can do it, then maybe there's hope for the world after all," he said with a smile. He was really cute when he smiled.

He sat down on the La-Z-Boy chair, released the handle, and lay back. His guitar was on his chest and he held it as though it were a lady. He flicked off the lamp next to him and turned on the TV, which was broadcasting snow.

"Do you mind if I leave the TV on?" he asked. "I like waking up to morning cartoons."

"Me, too," I said. "I like to watch *Super Friends* on Saturday mornings."

"Really?"

"Yeah."

"Who's your favorite superhero?" he asked.

"Well, on *Super Friends*, obviously it's Wonder Woman."

"The girl."

"She's called Wonder *Woman*."

"I like Aquaman," he said. "He can talk to fish and stuff."

"I wish I could talk to fish," I said. I was drifting off. I was dreaming. Then there was nothing, until someone was shaking me awake.

"Hey," Caleb said as he was leaning over me. "Yrena's on TV."

"What? No," I said. I was wide awake now because I heard the anchorperson say Yrena's name.

"*. . . Yrena Yusim, a Soviet teenager, has been missing from her Riverdale apartment since last night. The Soviet government is asking for help in bringing her back home. So far there is no evidence that this is a defection or a kidnapping, but authorities are not ruling out that possibility. The girl is scheduled to return to Russia next week.*"

"Oh my God," I said. I sat up. I stood up. I sat back down. I put my hands over my face.

"Hey, you're not going to cry, are you?" Caleb asked. I could sense him backing away a little bit because I was now the girl who was in his living room crying. It was like I had the plague or something.

"What am I going to do?"

"I dunno," Caleb said. "Go home now?"

"Maybe I should call my brother again," I said. "See if he knows what's going on."

"Sounds good to me." Caleb pointed me to the phone.

My fingers were shaking. They felt like they would get stuck in the rotary phone holes as I dialed.

I knew it was early. 7:15, according to the wall clock.

"You've reached Todd. Rhymes with *Zod*. Land of Nod. And alien pod. Leave your transmission at the tone. May the Force be with you."

"Todd. Are you there? Pick up."

I sat on the telephone stool and leaned my head against the glass of the door.

"Todd. It's Ro—"

The phone clicked as he picked up.

"Yo," Todd said. He had that groggy I-want-to-sleep-all-day tone. I couldn't tell whether it was because of Dungeons and Dragons or what was going on with Yrena.

Silence.

Then the phone clicked again.

"Did you hear that?" Todd asked.

"Do you hear me?" I asked back.

"Yeah. Yeah. Uh. Everyone is freaking out about that movie. Man, I am going to go see it again today for sure."

"What?" I asked. Why was he so weird? I didn't have time for his games. I opened my mouth to start reaming him out but he wouldn't let me get a word in edgewise.

"Uh, yeah, *Danielle*, I'm so happy you called me, and we're totally on. Hey, I was thinking of seeing *E.T.* again for sure."

"What? Todd?"

"I sure do like Steven Spielberg. I'd like to bring him roses. Hey, that's my sister's name, Danielle, *Rose*."

Then he hung up on me.

I started to tremble because I realized that it must be really bad over at the house. People must really be listening in to the telephone calls. Oh my God. My phone was being tapped. Or someone was in the room with him.

"What happened?" Caleb asked.

"My brother is freaking out. I think it must be bad over at the house."

"Bad like how?" Caleb asked.

"I don't know! KGB! CIA!"

"Okay, don't freak out on me. 'Cause if you freak out then I don't want to help you."

"Right." I took a breath.

"What did your brother say?"

"He talked about *E.T.*"

"Good movie."

"Do me a favor," I said. "Let's just not tell Yrena that she's a top story on the news. We'll just go to the march for a little while, and meanwhile I'll figure out how to get us home."

"You're a little radical, aren't you?" Caleb said. "Who knew?"

I shrugged. Maybe that *was* what I was now. A radical. I let that sit on me like a 1920s flapper's skullcap. It was snug and it fit okay for that moment. I was feeling pretty radical.

We woke the others up and we all ate cereal together.

Caleb kept quiet about the news, but I noticed that he kept glancing at me and giving me a look. I didn't know what the look meant. Was he giving me the eye? Did he want to say something to me? Was it a signal?

I'd have to get him alone and ask him. In the meantime, I made my face unreadable.

We returned to the Staten Island Ferry — this time in daylight — and headed back to the city. And as the skyline got larger, it looked gray and menacing, not as magical as it had under the cover of the dark night.

I had no idea what was waiting for us there.

The March

The sound was like a roar in the air when we emerged from underground.

"What is that noise?" I asked.

"It's the march!" Callisto said.

There were thousands of people all walking in the same direction, streaming up the streets. They were everywhere. Their voices singing, talking, humming, praying, their hearts beating, their feet walking, all together made the air buzz. And, amazingly, all of them had come together for one purpose: peace.

I ask you, how could you feel helpless against the bigness of the world with that kind of gathering?

I ask you, how could you not be swept away?

You couldn't.

We stepped into the stream of people heading toward the park, and I was glad that our voices made the crowd that much louder. I could almost hear the change in volume that our voices added.

I was glad of it.

"I thought that it would just be old hippies," Caleb said, looking around.

"Me, too," I told him.

"I am pleasantly surprised," he said.

It was an ocean of every kind of person you could possibly imagine. Everyone who made up New York City. Everyone who made up the world. Professionals, parents, children, punks, physicists, yuppies, artists, actors, firemen, dock workers, cabbies, teachers. Everyone. It was a people-watching paradise.

They all had signs.

PROFESSIONALS FOR A NUKE-FREE WORLD!

PARENTS FOR NO NUKES! NO WARS!

TEACH TOLERANCE! TEACH PEACE! TEACHERS SAY NO NUKES!

PUNKS FOR PEACE!

PHYSICISTS FOR ATOMS! NOT BOMBS!

GET ACTIVE! NOT RADIOACTIVE!

"Who is Ron?" Yrena asked, pointing to a sign that said THIS IS NOT A MOVIE, RON!

"Our president," Maurice said. "Ronald Reagan."

"He was a movie actor," I explained.

"Oh, I see—this is real life and not a movie, Ronald Reagan," she said, and then she laughed.

A huge blue whale balloon went by. It had a thought bubble over its head that said SAVE THE HUMANS.

"Ha!" I said, pointing it out to everyone.

"It's probably true that if whales could talk they would tell us to stop having nuclear bombs," Callisto said.

We all nodded.

"Those whales would definitely have something to say about it," I said.

"Too bad that's not in my skit," Caleb said. "Let's go, or I'll be late."

We pushed deeper into the thick of the crowd.

I felt as though I was a part of something bigger than myself. I looked around at the other people — some walked at our pace, some moved faster, and some took their time, but they were all like us. We smiled at them and they smiled at us, and embraced us as part of them. We shook our heads in approval back at them, and as we did, they welcomed us.

People even handed us signs to hold up.

Loving Arms, Not Nuclear Arms

Freeze the Arms Race

It's a World Emergency

The crowd thickened the closer we got to Central Park. We had our free arms linked together so that we didn't lose one another, and with our free hands we held up the signs. There were more people there than I'd ever seen in one place. More people on the streets than what I'd seen at the Macy's Thanksgiving Day Parade. There were people with bullhorns. There were people with banners that said No Nukes Now!

As we walked toward the park, I noticed that there were many people just watching us marchers walk by.

"How can they stand there?" I said. "We're not a parade!"

"Calm down there, radical," Caleb said. "They have the right to watch. Maybe they won't join us this time, but maybe next time."

"But we are walking for *them*. How can they not be moved by the message? The message that we all want to live?"

"I think some people just don't feel for the whole world," Caleb said.

"It's hard to feel for the whole world," Yrena observed.

"It's hard to even feel for your friends and family sometimes," I said. "But that doesn't mean you shouldn't try to."

Yrena seemed to be a bit overwhelmed by everything that was going on.

Some of the bystanders were not just watching us passively. They were yelling at us all as we walked by. There were people protesting the peace march. There were people screaming that *we* were the dangerously naive ones.

They yelled: *Peace is a Soviet weapon.*

They yelled: *The devil's headquarters is in Moscow.*

They yelled: *You cannot trust those who are evil. They have bullhorns.*

What they were yelling hurt us all, but Yrena was the hardest hit.

I looked at Yrena and I could see how upset she was. She

was holding on to her sign as though it were going to hold her upright. I could tell that she wanted to cry.

We all touched her nicely so that she knew that we felt terrible and that we did not feel as though she was evil at all.

"But who is a devil? Me? You? Them?" she asked.

The people lined up thought anyone who didn't think like them was the devil, and that was surely evil. But they were just scared, like we were.

"Those people yelling at us for marching are just as angry and upset as we are about nuclear bombs," I said.

"They feel that we are against real peace and that we are messing up their safety in this world," Caleb said.

"Isn't that weird?" Callisto said. "That two groups of people can feel so much like the other side is dangerous and naively misguided."

"That's why we're at war," Maurice said.

"Just keep walking," I said. "Don't listen to them."

"Propaganda," Yrena said. "It is just to make us seem like, what do you call it?"

"The Red Menace," I said.

"Yes. The Red Menace. We were not the only ones with bombs pointed. We were not the only ones who propagated this idea. Only you covered it up and call it being *free*."

"They're free to protest," Caleb said. "Just like we are."

"I'm not afraid to observe your protest rituals," Yrena said. "I don't hate you people. I like you."

"We don't hate you, either," Callisto said. "Obviously."

"Glad that's out of the way," Caleb said.

"Is it really hate?" I asked. "Is that what it is?"

"No," Yrena said. "It's not hate. It's not the *mes* and *yous*. When it is *me* and *you*, it is always fine."

"It's the *uses* and *thems*," I said.

"Why can't our countries get along?" Callisto asked. "I mean, why can't they see that having bombs pointed at each other is stupid? I can see it's stupid."

"I can see it's stupid, too," Yrena said.

"Even Reagan and Brezhnev can see that it's stupid," Maurice said.

"But they don't do anything about it," I said. "They just keep at it."

"Maybe they think that keeps it balanced?" Caleb said.

"But don't we ever figure it out?" Caitlin asked. "I mean, is there ever a point where we realize that we are all human beings and that life is precious?"

"No," I said. "No matter how many people speak up, people always hate."

"I hate haters," Callisto said.

"Me, too," Yrena said.

"I can't wait until I'm eighteen," I said, "so I can vote for change."

That's when Caleb punched me in the arm.

"You're so cool," he said.

And then he put his arm around my waist and squeezed

like he *liked* me. I felt a thrill and it was more than just from being in a crowd a half a million people strong.

The truth was, we were always in a sort of tentative balance with someone. Friends, even the best of friends, were always in danger of destroying each other. Alliances shifted and changed. People came together and fell apart.

It was all politics, except that in friendship we were held in balance by the heart and in the real world we were held in balance by the fact that there was a thing called MAD: Mutually Assured Destruction. So if one side attacked the other, the bombs from the other side were launched automatically, to assure that both sides were completely annihilated. It didn't surprise me that the acronym was MAD. That was mad. Pure. Crazy. Madness.

It made me look up at the sky. It made me see the world in a much more focused way.

"Do you really think there will be a nuclear war?" I asked Yrena. "I mean, it seems so hard to believe that we or you would do that."

"Hard to believe on a beautiful morning like this," Caleb said.

"I don't think that a bright day protects us from people whose hearts are immune to trust and filled with such darkness," Yrena said. "And sadly, bombs are incapable of having anything, even a truly fine feeling, touch them."

That made me have goose bumps. That made me want to fight harder for all that is good in the world. That made me want to bring my friends in closer to me. That made me want to pump my fist harder into the air.

As we walked, the crowd separated and walked around a spot on the street. On the ground were chalk outlines of bodies painted black. The result was that it looked as though only people's shadows had been left behind.

"They said that's what happens," Caleb said. "In seventh grade we read this book on Hiroshima and Nagasaki and there was a picture of someone's shadow sitting on the steps of a bank. That's all that was left of him."

"Oh yeah," Callisto said. "I remember wondering if when you melt, does it hurt?"

"It must hurt," Caitlin said.

"It must be something terrible," Yrena said.

"How could a society think that they are a better people?" I asked. "That they think a better way? That they live a better way? And that, because they are better, they are allowed to kill other people?" I asked.

"It's the oldest story in the book," Callisto said.

"As if we live any differently. As if we all aren't just trying to put food on the table, and fall in love, and get through the day," Maurice said.

"How long can we stay right on the brink of hating each other?" Caitlin said.

"They said that the Doomsday Clock is almost at midnight. We are hovering on the edge of destruction," Caleb said.

"We do it because you do it," Yrena said. "And you do it

because we do it. Everyone does it because everyone else does it. As you said, it's the oldest story in the book."

"That doesn't mean it's a good story," I said.

Once we got inside of Central Park, there were a lot of policemen, on foot and on horses.

A march volunteer handed us two silver balloons and told us not to let them go until we were told to.

"How will we know when?" I asked the volunteer.

"You'll know," she said. Each balloon said GOOD-BYE, NUCLEAR WEAPONS.

There were vendors at the entrance to the park, hawking No Nukes stuff.

"I want one of those T-shirts," Yrena said.

It was white with a pink-and-red stripe and a little sun on it, and said REVERSE THE ARMS RACE!

We all wanted one.

"Well, Yrena has to get a T-shirt," I said. We pooled our money together to buy her one.

After what seemed like much longer than needed to be because of all the people, we got to the rock, where the party had been the night before. A bunch of people from Performing Arts were there.

"Hey!" Elliot Waldman said. "Glad you got here."

"Hi," Caitlin said. She was blushing.

Caleb left us and joined the others in the skit. After about fifteen minutes, Elliot stood up and gathered a crowd around the base of the rock and announced the Performing Arts Revolutionary Players.

"Here is the truth," Caleb said in his old-timey emcee voice. "We are always thirty minutes away from total destruction."

And then they launched into their skit. I am Russia. I am America. Fisticuffs. Girls as bombs. Bomb noises. Everyone fell down and melted from a nuclear attack and while they lay there, they began to sing "America the Beautiful" and the whole crowd joined in.

We clapped. But some adults said that it was shameful that kids were being brought up to be so anti-American.

"Anti-American!" Caleb yelled back at some older guy. "What are you doing here then?"

"Relax," I said. I put my hand on his shoulder.

"Hey, just because we had a moment before doesn't mean anything," he said, shaking me off.

He pushed by me and went to join the other actors behind the rock. Presumably to get stoned.

"Hey, sorry about that," Caitlin said.

"He can be really sensitive about his art," Callisto said. "I think he just got upset that people got upset."

"Well, I liked it," I said. "I thought it was great."

"Yrena!"

Like a miracle, we had found Free. He was walking by the rock and saw us.

"Free!" Yrena said as she and the others emerged right behind us.

"Hey! Wicked! You guys made it!" Free said.

Yrena went straight up to Free and kissed him right on the lips. He looked a little surprised but also really happy.

"Free," Yrena said. "I have something to tell you. I will be back in Moscow on Friday."

"What?" he said.

"I am moving back home to Moscow," Yrena said.

"This is her only day out," I said, trying to come to Yrena's rescue. She smiled at me, and I could tell she appreciated it.

"Really?" Free said. "You're going back to the USSR?"

"*Da*," she said. "Friday."

"So, like, you're not someone who defected? You're, like, really Russian?" Free said.

"I am not a defector. I'm a Soviet citizen," Yrena said.

"Wow. I thought you were just an immigrant or something," he said.

"No. I am a Soviet citizen."

Caleb came back out and came straight up to me.

"That was lame," he said. "I was lame. No one even cared about our piece."

"I cared," I said.

"I know," he said. And then he smiled at me. "Friends?"

I nodded.

"Let's go see some of the bands," I said. Then I turned to

Free, who had just come up for air after kissing Yrena some more. "I thought you had a whole big group coming from Science."

"Nope," Free said. "I'm the only one who showed up. I have a social conscience."

"I can't believe you actually found us," I said.

"I talked to a cop and he said there are at least five hundred thousand people here," Free said.

"That is a lot of people," I said.

"Yes, but we found you," Yrena said. "We were looking for you!"

"Do you think this is what Woodstock was like?" Callisto asked. We started walking toward the Great Lawn.

"My parents took me to Woodstock," Free said.

"Really?" Caleb said. "That's kind of cool."

"What is Woodstock?" Yrena asked Free.

"It was a three-day rock concert," Free explained.

"A big love-in," Callisto said.

"Love-in. I like that," Yrena said.

"At least your parents went to Woodstock. My dad's a jazz musician; he doesn't know anything about rock and roll," Caleb said.

"Yeah, my parents are a mess, but they love rock and roll. They're both here at this protest. Just not together."

I realized that I liked my parents and my family. They were not extreme. They were not clueless. They were not cool, but they were not uncool. They were normal. In the middle. Just fine. That made me kind of happy. Like, at least I didn't have to worry about having crappy parents.

James Taylor started to sing, and I leaned back into Caleb's chest. I don't know why I did it, but I did, and then he had his arms around my waist. Maurice and Callisto were dancing in time to the music. Callisto knew the words to the song and so she was singing along, but she was doing it low and in Maurice's ear. I noticed that Yrena and Free were hovering near each other, and then I watched as Free did the pin on Yrena as she leaned up against a tree that we were next to.

I was with a group of people who I thought could be my real friends.

A man got onstage and said, "Three thousand of you have silver balloons. On those balloons it says GOOD-BYE, NUCLEAR WEAPONS."

Everyone cheered.

"All together now, starting on ten," he said.

After the crowd counted down, we let go of the two balloons we had, and they joined the thousands of other balloons that rose and floated into the air like a reverse snow. They floated up into the gray day.

We all breathed in and out as one as we watched them become smaller and smaller until they were impossible to see in the sky. We hoped with all our might that we really were saying good-bye to nuclear bombs. Because that would have been the best news.

More people got on the stage and gave speeches. One of them told us exactly what would happen if a nuclear bomb hit Central Park right that minute. It would vaporize everyone within six miles.

It was terrible.

Why did we have weapons that could do that? It was inhuman.

We were trembling.

We wanted to do something that would make us feel better.

And just in the moment when I felt surrounded by friends, the music started again. There I was in the arms of a cute boy, happier than I'd ever been. You had to embrace life in order to fight death. You had to grab hold of joy in order to fend off destruction. You had dance wildly instead of standing still.

At the moment when I felt right with everything, when the music in my heart was just right, I knew what I had to do.

"Yrena, I have to tell you something," I said.

And then I told her about the news report. And about talking to my brother on the phone. And about the clicks.

She stood there and she stared at me. Her eyes got a far-away look in them.

Yrena nodded.

"Yes," she said. "I suspected that would happen."

"We should go home soon," I said.

Yrena nodded, and I didn't feel anxious anymore.

Rita Marley took the stage and began to sing. Her voice slipped around us with love and peace.

The last song that was sung as they closed the protest was "Give Peace a Chance." We sang and swayed, everyone's voices lifting to the sky like wishes. My friends and I were all arms and limbs and togetherness as we sung. I stood closest to Caleb and Yrena. I couldn't tell where my body started and where theirs ended.

And then it was done.

"Time to go home," I said.

We left the park with all the others, and there was such a sense of camaraderie between us all. Not just me and my new friends, but between me and the whole world.

As Yrena and I climbed on to the 1 train heading back to the Bronx, it was almost as though we had forgotten that it was forever good-bye.

The thing was, saying good-bye is actually too hard. So sometimes you just don't. You just keep listening to the music. You just keep swaying side to side. You just keep going until the day is over. I couldn't see how a person said good-bye when it was forever good-bye. It would be slow and sad. It would be painful and foggy. It made no sense. Like being underwater. Or seeing things flicker and extinguish.

We were tired. We wanted to go home. We talked all the way about everything that had happened that night. About what we could do to top it. About how we would hang out every single day before she left. About Free's kisses and about Caleb's holding my hand on the way through the crowd.

When we got to the bottom of our street, humming one of the Pete Seeger songs, trying to remember the words, and looking for a stick of gum in our purses because we realized we hadn't brushed our teeth in over a day, we learned that going home wasn't going to be as easy as we thought.

They were waiting to grab us as soon as we came in sight of them.

Men in suits.

We didn't see them at first. All I heard was a word: "You!" Then a snap as one of these men, CIA by his eyebrows, unhooked something from his belt. At first I thought it was his gun, but then I saw that he was speaking into his walkie-talkie.

"I've got them," he said.

There was then some Russian spoken by one of the other men, softly, like the lullaby that Yrena had sung to us. It was Yrena. She was talking to me, telegraphing a message.

"But I don't understand," I said.

"*Da*," she said, and turned. "Take off your shoes."

She was taking off her shoes, stepping out of them. I did the same because she had asked me to.

"We're just going home," I said as the next pair of suits

approached us. They were not smiling. They were angry and yelling in Russian. They seemed to be in disagreement with the first pair of suits about who had authority.

"We live just up the street," I said. I was trying to be helpful. But the suits closest to me put their fingers in my face, shushing me.

The man closest to me nodded to the other men — KGB, if I went by his eyebrows — who were escorting Yrena away from me.

No one noticed about our shoes. Yrena was walking barefoot up the hill. She looked back over her shoulder to me and smiled.

"Come with me, please," the man who stayed with me said. His arm was holding my shoulder so tightly, I couldn't go in any other direction than where he led me.

I had to Nancy Drew what she was trying to tell me with that look. I wanted to tell her that she was leaving her shoes behind, but something stopped me when I stared at the shoes. In hers I could see the piece of paper with the address the waiter had given her, folded up and springing out from under the tongue like a small ladder stopped by the laces.

"Can I get my shoes?" I asked.

The man nodded and we went to retrieve my shoes. I slipped Yrena's on my feet. They were too big and I had to clench my toes to keep them on as I walked.

The Girls Who Came In from the Cold

Isn't it funny how you could know a person for fewer than twenty-four hours and know everything about them? Know someone better than you've ever known anyone? Know when they are being themselves or not? Know someone better than you even know yourself?

They came and took us away from each other and interviewed us separately.

They asked me so many questions.

"How long have you known her?"

"Who instigated the incident?"

"Did she force you to go along with her?"

"Would you say that you were under duress?"

"Would you say that you felt your life was in danger?"

"So you don't really know her at all?"

I wanted to say:

"I've known her for forever."

"We both decided to have an adventure together!"

"We are not our countries!"

But the lawyer said I should keep my mouth shut. He said that it would be better for me to emphasize that I had only met her on Friday.

So that's what I did.

And that's what made me a traitor.

After it was all over, the CIA let my parents and my brother into the interrogation room.

"Why didn't you girls just come home right away?" Now it was my dad who was interrogating me. The lines in his forehead when he furrowed his brow were so deep, they looked like canals.

"I don't know," I said.

The truth was that we were never *not* going to go home. We kept meaning to go home, and then it just got later and later. And then it got harder and harder. And at some point during all that, we started to have fun. But how do you say that? How do you say that staying out had suddenly become more important than the consequences? Because it was the only time. It was the only night.

Nobody understood that.

I wanted to tell them that I would never give that night up because even though I was going to be in more trouble than I had ever known, I had made friends for life.

But my mom must have known that, because she sat next to me and smoothed my hair and smiled at me.

"What did you girls do?" she asked.

"We went to a party," I said. "We went to a party and we had fun."

"That's what you keep saying," my dad intoned.

It didn't matter if I said it a million times. It didn't matter if it was true. I felt like he was never going to believe me. He was never going to let me forget the fact that the authorities were in his house, questioning him and his politics that morning. That he was just a guy who didn't vote for Reagan, who fell asleep during the eleven o'clock news, and who didn't ever think about or want to think about the Cold War as being something that affected him in any way.

"Dan, relax," my mom said. "Rose is okay."

I laid my head on the table.

"I'm done talking," I said.

"Rose," she said, "you girls did the right thing by coming home."

"I really never meant to be any trouble," I said.

"I know, baby," my mom said, and hugged me again. She put her arms around me and held me tight, like she loved me something fierce.

I looked up at my dad and it looked like he wanted to say something to me. It looked like he wanted to say *I'm sorry*.

I took my sweater off the back of the chair and lost my balance a little as I stood up.

My brother caught my elbow and helped me keep steady.

Just like he was at the bus stop, he was there to walk me out of the federal building.

I was free to go. I was on my way home.

The CIA drove me and my family back to my house in Riverdale.

I couldn't bear to look at my parents, and even Todd knew to let me be, so I looked outside the window and stared out across the river at New Jersey. The George Washington Bridge flew by. Cars were going places. A Circle Line boat was sailing on the Hudson River, full of tourists. People were just doing their thing.

One day you could be a normal girl. In America. Free. Your blood ran red, white, and blue. And then Monday morning, you were alluded to in the *New York Times* as an "unspecified international incident."

My parents were deathly quiet next to me and I knew I would never be the same.

I was still a ballerina. That would never change. And somehow I was surer of it than before. I was a ballerina.

But I was also a girl who was under suspicion of consorting with an enemy of the state.

I looked out my window across the driveway at Yrena's house. I thought it was going to be dark and empty, like they'd been removed in the middle of the night, but the light was on in Yrena's room.

I could see that it was full of boxes and everything looked bare.

I thought maybe she wasn't there. I thought maybe she was already gone halfway across the world. I decided that I wouldn't draw my curtains closed. I just kept looking over at her window, wondering what she was doing. If she was okay. If she was in a lot of trouble. If she was thinking about me. And then suddenly she walked into her room. I was just standing there, surprised to see her. I wondered if she would look up. There was no way to yell over at her without getting us both into trouble. There were suits stationed in front of both of our houses.

Finally she did it. She looked up.

I waved. So did she. We smiled. But it broke my heart. We couldn't even say anything to each other. This was terrible. Then I got an idea. I motioned for her to wait a second. She nodded that she would. I got a marker and a stack of paper.

ARE YOU OK? I wrote it down and pressed the note up against the glass, hoping that she could read it. Hoping that she could see it. Hoping that she could read English as well as she spoke it.

She smiled and nodded.

DO YOU GO HOME TOMORROW?

She nodded.

I copied down the Cyrillic from the paper in the shoe, hoping that she could read it.

She gave me a thumbs-up.

I wrote, again.

I'M SO GLAD THAT WE BECAME FRIENDS.

She bobbed her head up and down furiously. I could see that she was crying. She blew me some kisses. I blew her some, too. I saw her turn her head and say something. Then I saw her mom walk into the room. Her mom looked out the window and saw me. I saw her face soften, like she felt bad, but she had to do what she had to do.

I waved. I waved to make sure my good-bye was seen. Yrena lifted her hand up, too. She waved good-bye. Good-bye. Good-bye.

Yrena's mom went to the window and pulled down the shade.

That was it.

Good-bye.

Wednesday

My parents said that I didn't have to go to school until I was ready to. Part of me wanted to just curl up in a ball and stay in bed for a year, but I knew that I had to go in. I couldn't stay home.

On Wednesday I made my way downtown.

I saw Callisto and Caitlin hanging out in their usual spot, leaning against the brick wall below the window that looked into the office. Caleb was with them. It filled me with joy to see them all there. They didn't see me as I walked up to them. They were in deep conversation; sometimes they laughed, sometimes they furrowed their brows. As I got closer, I noticed that Maurice was standing with them, sharing his coffee with Callisto.

Caleb saw me first.

He smiled. He raised his hand up. But then he thought about it for a second, scowled as per usual, and turned away from me in his broody way.

He was being cold and aloof, but I could tell, because I

was a dancer and I could read the movements in a person's body, that Caleb really wanted to run to me. He was holding himself back. And that made me feel so good. I wanted to run to him. But I held myself back, too.

I walked over to my group of friends.

"Hi," I said.

"We were worried about you when you didn't come to school," Maurice said.

"And then when we read about the international incident in the *Times* yesterday," Callisto said, "we realized that the incident was you."

"Are you okay?" Caitlin asked.

I was about to start crying or turn away because I couldn't handle the fact that this crazy, huge thing had happened and I didn't know where to put it. The whole thing seemed unreal, but these people knew that it had happened. We were all witnesses to the moment.

Caleb looked at me from under his bangs. He wasn't being broody. He was being shy. He didn't say anything and I couldn't speak.

And then Caleb didn't need to say anything because he made a move toward me and he put his arms around me and hugged me so tightly that I felt like he was hugging the very me that hides inside. After a moment, Caitlin, Callisto, and Maurice piled on, too.

"Are you okay?" Callisto asked me when Caleb finally let me go.

"Shaky," I said.

"Yrena?" Callisto said.

"Gone," I said. "Or going soon."

Everyone's face went grim.

"That's so sucky," Caitlin said.

"I wish things could be different," Maurice said.

"I really wish that our countries didn't hate each other so much that Yrena couldn't come back and visit or something," Callisto said.

"Hey, guys, I just wanted to say . . ." I started.

"I just want you all to know . . ." I started again.

"It's just that it really meant a lot . . ." I started a third time.

I wanted to say it. I wanted to say thank you, but I didn't know how.

"Hey," Callisto said, stubbing out her clove cigarette. "No sweat. You'd do the same for us."

And she was right. I would have in a heartbeat.

"So, I'm going to go in to warm up for class," Maurice said to me. "You wanna join me?"

I nodded.

"Great!" he said. "See you at lunch, Callisto?"

"Yep," she said, and then they kissed quickly.

"I have a free period right before lunch," Caleb said to me. "I was going to go get a sandwich at Le Café. Can I get you something?"

"Yeah, a plain yogurt with some honey?"

"You got it," he said, and he was still holding my hand right up until Maurice and I headed inside. The downstairs was quiet, but as we headed up to the dance department, it got louder. There was music and people talking, and my classmates weren't just warming up in a boring, repetitive way. They were warming up and practicing combinations and they were trying out different kinds of moves, creating their own dances. Not just ballet or modern. They were free dancing, which was a kind of dancing that I could do and not be the worst at.

They kind of stopped and looked at me when I came in all dressed and ready to work. They looked at me as though I was a stranger . . . because mostly I was.

I was worried that I wasn't going to fit in after all and that this was a stupid mistake. But Maurice took me by the elbow and led me into the center of the room and started to stretch next to me. I followed his lead and started stretching, too.

Hang in there, Rose, I thought. *Just make it through the day.* The bell rang, meaning it was time for my first class: ballet.

Ms. Zina's cane banged on the floor, announcing the start of class. She began counting out the time as we did our barre exercises. One, two, three. One, two, three. And plié. And relevé. And coupé.

"Now, first group, the combination from last week," Ms. Zina said.

I watched Maurice and group one do the combination.

"Group two." Ms. Zina banged her cane on the ground.

I turned and faced the mirror.

Preparation.

And go.

My heart went straight to my feet.

I was a dancer.